SUMMER

A SURREAL STORIES COLLECTION

DEAN WESLEY SMITH

WMG
PUBLISHING

ALSO BY DEAN WESLEY SMITH

COLD POKER GANG

Kill Game

Cold Call

Calling Dead

Bad Beat

Dead Hand

Freezeout

Ace High

Burn Card

Heads Up

Ring Game

Bottom Pair

Case Card

THUNDER MOUNTAIN

Thunder Mountain

Monumental Summit

Avalanche Creek

The Edwards Mansion

Lake Roosevelt

Warm Springs

Melody Ridge

Grapevine Springs

The Idanha Hotel

The Taft Ranch

Tombstone Canyon

Dry Creek Crossing

Hot Springs Meadow

Green Valley

SEEDERS UNIVERSE

Dust and Kisses: A Seeders Universe Prequel Novel

Against Time

Sector Justice

Morning Song

The High Edge

Star Mist

Star Rain

Star Fall

Starburst

Rescue Two

CONTENTS

BRYANT STREET

SUMMER

INTRODUCTION

IT ALL MIGHT BE SEASONABLE

For years and years, actually decades and decades, I kept saying that one day I would do a Bryant Street collection or two, and I just never got around to it.

Finally, in the winter of 2023, I decided it was time and told the fine folks at WMG Publishing I was going to do this. Stephanie Writt came up with the cool street-sign logo and I was off.

I thought it would be cool to have Bryant Street be a television series with four seasons of ten episodes each season. (For those of you who don't know, a short story usually has enough story for a single thirty-minute episode of anything on television.)

So I sent the idea of four seasons to Stephanie at WMG and back comes the four wonderful covers using seasons of the year. I was about to object when it dawned on me that four seasons of the year would be a lot easier to explain than four seasons of a television show.

And these would act as ten episodes of a season, but each season would start on the first day of the named season. A full year of Bryant Street.

So I started with the forty stories together and then put them into seasons.

Often a story is set in the title season. Or the story is dark like winter. Or hot like summer.

Or a character in the last days of their lives like winter, or fading like fall. In one way or another, all the stories fit into a season.

But think of them like ten episodes per run. The winter season run, the spring season run, and so on.

Sort of like ten episodes per season of a series like *The Twilight Zone* television series used to be. Every episode different, yet every episode set on Bryant Street.

Smith's STORIES

DEAN WESLEY SMITH

WRONG TURN
A Bryant Street Short Story

WRONG TURN

Bryant Street, where things just never seem right, never work right, never exist as expected.

I created Bryant Street a long time ago when Stephen King said writers should write about what scares them. Subdivisions terrify me at a deep level, so I created Bryant Street.

I lived this story far too many times in subdivisions. Luckily escaped with my life each time, but only barely.

Patrick Cutler was lost.

That simple. He was lost in his own subdivision.

He eased his rented Ford coupe over to the edge of the curb and stopped. He kicked up the air-conditioning a touch to fight off not only the heat of the late-July day outside of Las Vegas, but also his sweating from worry.

How could he be lost? He had bought the house on Bryant Street six months ago, spent a month in it in February, then had gone north to his home in Portland.

But he had a three-day business conference down here and even though he hated the intense summer heat here, he figured he might as well stay at his own place.

But he had never noticed when he bought the place and lived here that every house in this massive subdivision looked almost identical. Especially in the shimmering waves of heat.

All the homes were desert brown stucco, tile roofs, desert low-water landscaping that all looked identical. All had two-car garages, all had windows covered in blinds, and all had large numbers on the side near the garage that seemed to make no sense at all. When he thought the numbers were going up, he would go around a shallow corner and suddenly they would be different numbers and heading down in count.

And the street signs in this subdivision seemed to be almost non-existent, as if the designers had wanted people to get lost. And no street was straight. All of them curved one way or another, moving up and over small ridgelines and then back into shallow valleys, all the while the streets changed names as it turned out, without warning.

Patrick hadn't given that any thought at all. He loved his home outside of Portland, but the last few winters had been too cold for him and since he liked Las Vegas and could work from anywhere, he had bought a second home here.

He had heard when he bought the place that this subdivision alone had over four thousand homes in it. One of the largest built in the Las Vegas area. He just never realized how massive an area four thousand homes covered.

So for the last thirty minutes he had been just driving, looking for any sign of his house. And now he wasn't even sure he could get out of the subdivision to even try to start over.

He remembered that to find his house, he went in from a main road, turned right, then two quick lefts, and his house would be five houses down on the right.

Easy.

But something had gone wrong or he had driven right past his place and not noticed it.

Or he had come in off the main road on the wrong road.

Didn't matter. He was lost now.

He finished off the last of his bottle of water and looked around.

Granted it was in the middle of the day and the temperature wasn't looking back at one hundred, but he hadn't seen one bit of movement. Not even another car moving.

A lot of people had homes here. Something should be moving.

But it looked like most of the homes weren't even being lived in, like his. More than likely these were all owned by snowbirds, people like him who went south when the snow started to fly.

Now he wished he had just stayed in the conference

hotel. If he could make his way out of here that was where he was headed now.

He felt trapped in his rental car by the heat, so he got it moving forward again, driving slowly, watching numbers and street signs and looking for any road that looked to be a main road to get out of this maze.

Nothing.

Thirty minutes later, he stopped his car again, this time right in the middle of the road.

His address was fourteen-fourteen Bryant Street. How tough would that be to find?

He pulled out his phone and tried putting in that address again, to show him where it was from his location. He had already tried that twice, without luck.

This time his home address showed up and showed his location a good mile away, the symbol for him in his car blinking.

He held the phone in one hand while driving again, heading in the general direction. He seemed to make progress, winding along the streets.

Then at about a half mile from his home he ended up going back in the other direction because the road had just gradually turned on him.

He tried two side-streets, but both ended up to be cul-de-sacs.

Finally the third street got him going back in slightly the right direction. But it soon turned as well.

He stopped his car again and switched direction apps on

his phone, using one that brought up written directions to get to his address from his location.

It had now been over an hour and he still had not seen another person moving. It was starting to get creepy.

And even with the air-conditioning, he was thirsty.

The directions from the app seemed to go on forever. He took a deep breath and followed the first turn instructed, then the second, then the third.

He carefully followed every direction until suddenly the directions made no sense. The street name wasn't right, the distance off.

Had he made a wrong turn?

He went back to the previous app to see his location.

He was farther away, if that was possible.

He banged his hand on the steering wheel and went back to the app with directions and carefully typed in his home address and again asked for directions from his location.

Once again he followed the directions exactly, making sure every turn was right, that every street was right, that every distance was right.

Until it wasn't.

On the other app it showed him to be back almost in the same position that he had been when he first logged on.

"Screw this," he said.

He typed in the address of the conference hotel down on The Strip and asked for directions. The least he could do was get out of this maze.

Again the directions seemed to go on and on, so he carefully followed them, making one turn, going twenty houses on a gently turning street, making another turn.

Thirty more minutes he stopped and shut down the app, then brought it back up and asked for the same directions again.

He was no closer than he had been when he started. The stupid subdivision roads had just kept him circling around and back.

He clicked to another app on his phone and asked for a map of the area.

It showed the maze of streets with two major streets running along both sides. He seemed to be in the very middle of the maze, from what he could tell from the map.

He got a distant blue mountain in his sights and decided he would do this the old-fashioned way.

Keeping that mountain in sight, he just kept making turns to go toward it, even though the roads turned him back around numbers of times.

Still no other cars, no people, no house that looked lived in.

Then the worst thing he could ever imagine happened.

His car sputtered and steam started to pour out from under the hood. He had been driving so slowly, the air-conditioning on high, he had overheated the car in the intense heat.

He looked quickly around in front of him for any sign of shade.

Nothing. Just concrete driveways and streets and desert lawns.

He pulled over and shut off his car.

The intense silence slammed into him and the heat hit him almost instantly.

He was in trouble.

Big trouble.

He grabbed his phone and called 911.

"What is your emergency?"

"My name is Patrick Cutler. I am completely lost and my car has overheated on Hudson Street in the Frontier Subdivision. I have no water and no shelter. I'm going to need help quickly."

"Find shade if you can," the operator said. "Do you have water?"

"No," Patrick said. "I am in a rental car and haven't had anything to drink for hours now."

"Stay on the line," the operator said. "I will send help."

"Thank you," Patrick said.

He pushed open the door and the oven-like heat off the pavement hit him like a hammer and took his breath away. It had to be hot enough to cook something quickly on this pavement.

He could feel the heat of the pavement through his leather dress shoes as he climbed out of the car. He had no doubt that if he stopped walking his feet would burn.

"Help is on the way," the operator said.

"Thank you," Patrick said. "I'm in front of a house with the numbers 21202 on the front. I'm going to go see if they have a covered patio in the back."

"Understood," the operator said. "I'll have the officer

have his siren going so you can come back around to the street."

Patrick moved through a side gate of the house and toward the back. There was a patio, but it was mostly in sunlight.

He went up to the big sliding glass door and knocked. As he expected, there was no one home.

He glanced at the time on his phone. He had been lost for almost three hours. How was that even possible?

He leaned against the side of the building in a tiny sliver of shade, but it didn't feel like it was helping at all.

"Mr. Cutler, how are you doing?"

"Not very well," he said, telling the operator the truth. "I feel slightly dizzy."

"Can you lean against something that is not in the sun?"

"That's what I am doing," Patrick said. "How long?"

"It should only be a few minutes," the operator said. "Listen for the siren."

"I will," he said. "Thank you."

He stood against the building, looking at the stark desert landscaping of the back yard, the wooden plank fence, and that damned blue mountain off in the distance.

Around him nothing moved.

Not even a slight breeze.

Just total silence and heat.

Three hours without water, even in the air-conditioning, had dried him out. He knew he was going to be in trouble very quickly if help didn't arrive.

Finally, he heard the siren off in the distance.

"I can hear a siren," he said to the operator. "I'm going back toward my car."

"Good," the operator said.

But by the time he got out in front of the house, the sound of the siren had faded and was gone.

Then he heard it again.

He went up to the front porch of the house to stand in a tiny bit of shade there.

"I don't hear it anymore," he said.

"The officer is having some trouble," the operator said. "I am sending a second car now."

"Lost?" Patrick asked.

"It seems like he might be," the operator said.

Patrick laughed softly.

He could feel his energy drifting away. He had to do something and do it quickly.

"Operator, I am going to go back around the house here," he said. "And see if I can break a small window and get in. I need water and shade desperately. I will repay the owners for the damage."

"Understood," she said.

He half expected her to argue against doing that, but seems she understood clearly his situation.

He went around the house again and managed to find a rock large enough to break a window he thought he might be able to climb through.

Then he heard the siren again.

"I can hear the police," he said to the operator. "They seem to be getting closer."

"Good, go back to the front."

He did as she instructed, putting the rock down where he had found it. He was staggering now, through. And his phone said he had been in the heat for going on forty minutes since his car broke down.

The siren was loud, and what seemed like a block over.

"They are one block over from me," he said to the operator.

Patrick listened as the siren went past him a block away and faded.

Then another siren started up about five or six blocks away and that one went past him about two blocks behind the house.

"Both of them missed me," he said.

"They are working their way toward you," she said. "Just hold on."

He felt extremely dizzy, so he moved over to the small front steps on the house and sat down, leaning his head against the door.

"Not doing well," he managed to say to the operator.

"Hold on, Mr. Cutler," she said. "I'm tracing your cell phone and we are sending an emergency medical helicopter to your location."

Again a siren passed behind the house he was sitting in front of.

Another siren was two or three blocks away now.

Both officers seemed to be as lost as he had been.

It sure seemed this subdivision didn't much like him.

He tried to stand. He had to get around back and get inside and he had to do it now.

His legs wouldn't hold him and he remained sitting on the front steps.

He closed his eyes and let the faint blackness come up. He was so damned tired, he didn't much care anymore.

His last thought as the blackness took him was him wondering if the people who lived here ever got lost.

And that if he survived this, he would most certainly sell his house on Bryant Street.

If any real estate agent could find it.

Dean Wesley Smith
USA Today Bestselling Writer
For Your Consideration
A Bryant Street Story

FOR YOUR CONSIDERATION

Sometimes, what we all wish for can happen in the Twilight Zone.

Other times, our wishes come true on just a simple suburban street.

Caro Rosefield must investigate a very strange foreclosed home. A nightmare or maybe a new future?

On Bryant Street, anything seems possible. And anything can happen.

ONE

Caro Rosefield parked his rented Chevy Suburban near the curb of the quiet suburban street in a newer subdivision on the edge of the urban sprawl of Boise, Idaho. He left the engine running to keep the air-conditioning on since the temperature outside had just gone past one hundred and he didn't do well with heat. It made him light-headed and often sick.

The forecast for the Boise Valley was even hotter tomorrow. He hated July in general and he really hated it here in city plopped between a desert and a mountain.

He had his suit jacket in the back seat, his briefcase on the passenger floor, and the foreclosure paperwork for the house he was parked in front of on the seat beside him. Usually he never did anything without that jacket on, but it was just too hot to wear.

A couple of his friends teased him that since he had finished college he was never seen out of a suit. And dressing down for him was taking off the jacket. Caro had laughed at the ribbing, but it had hit home.

He didn't used to be like this. He liked backwoods biking and playing softball. But he'd been so busy lately, he couldn't drag his six-foot frame even out to see his oldest daughter play softball. He kept his hair short now, but in college it had been long, and now he was even getting a pot gut from sitting so much, something he hated but couldn't seem to find the time to do anything about.

He had three homes in this city his employer, Secured Construction and Management, wanted him to deal with. They had bought hundreds of foreclosed homes around the west. And were buying more every day for next to nothing and then flipping them. They were making money off the misery of families who had lost everything.

His job was to get the foreclosed homes in shape to sell. He was what they called "Shoes on the ground."

After he got these three homes here worked around, he could be back on the plane and out of this heat, back to his home in Portland, Oregon, where the normal color was green instead of dried brown.

He hated being away from his home and his family so much, especially his two daughters. They were getting to that age where things were changing every day, and if he blinked twice, they would be grown and gone and he will have missed them growing up completely.

He hated that the most about this job, but in these times, any job was a good job. Someone had to pay the mortgage and buy the clothes.

He checked the address on the paperwork one more time, then studied the split-level home that was his assignment at the moment. Nice home, about four thousand square feet, two levels, three bathrooms, large lot, two-car garage.

But this house looked to be a problem. A huge problem in fact. In three years of getting repossessed houses ready to show for sale for his company, he had never seen anything like what he was seeing now.

The house was already perfect.

In fact, the first time he had spotted the address, he figured he was on the wrong street.

But he wasn't. The house was 2761 Bryant Street.

He was on Bryant Street. Right town, right state, right legal description, everything. And the house had 2761 in clear numbers on the siding near the front door.

He picked up the stack of white papers and checked the address one more time.

Yup. That was the exact address on the papers that said this house used to belong to a couple named Davis that had lost it to First Trust Equity a year ago. First Trust Equity had then gone out of business and sold the house to his company four months ago. He had been put on the job to get the house ready to sell. He was to hire a team of local contractors and cleaners, get it into shape, clear out any signs of the previous owners who had lost the home, and then get the property listed with a local reality company.

But this house was clearly not empty as it was supposed to be.

The lawn had been freshly mowed and a paint truck was parked in the driveway. A paint crew of three men was actively working on a new coat of tan paint.

He had heard of people squatting in empty, bank-owned properties before, but never painting them. Something was very, very wrong here and he had a hunch he wasn't going to figure it out quickly.

In fact, more than likely this problem might be something for the lawyers to untangle.

Someone, somewhere, had screwed up and he was about to tell that fact to the fine people in this well-kept home that that they clearly cared for.

Damn he didn't want to do that. He wasn't supposed to

deal with people other than painters and cleaners and real estate agents. Never owners or squatters.

He had heard of things like this, just never been a part of it before.

He wished on this hot July afternoon, he wasn't a part of it now.

TWO

He glanced down the road. Four homes had sale signs in yards and all four seemed empty, lawns not watered or cut, and one empty house two doors down the street had a garage door that looked like it needed replaced. None of those homes were his concern. At least this trip. The way housing prices were dropping in this city, he had no doubt he would be back.

He hoped that next trip it wouldn't be so damned hot.

The house two doors up the street was the kind of place he expected to find here at 2761 Bryant Street. Not a well-kept two-story being freshly painted.

He leaned back into the blowing stream of air-conditioning and studied the place. Clearly the water was on since the lawn was a lush green and the power was turned on as well, since one of the painters had a compressor plugged in and working.

Water and power companies did not do that for squatters, only homeowners who could actually prove ownership.

"Oh, damn," he said to himself. "What a mess."

He let the cool air blow over him for another moment, then said, "Better get this over with."

He shut off the car and decided to just leave his jacket in the back seat. He even left the paperwork on the seat and just took his company business card with him. He had a hunch this wouldn't go well and he would be on the phone in a few minutes letting the company lawyers sort it all out.

He climbed out into the hot afternoon air. The heat wrapped around him like a choking rope that made his throat dry and his skin feel like it was flaking off.

His sweat didn't even last on his forehead it was so dry and hot.

How could anyone live in this kind of heat?

He headed for the front door, feeling like he was in a modern *Twilight Zone* episode. He had spent a lot of nights in hotel rooms watching old episodes of that show.

He could almost imagine Rod Serling standing off to one side of the freshly-mowed yard, smoking a cigarette, looking at the camera, saying, "For your consideration, one Mr. Caro Rosefield, hard worker, by-the-numbers kind of man, now faced with a dilemma pitting a corporation against a family's home. Mr. Caro Rosefield, the first shot of a war that can be seen being waged every day, not in the *Twilight Zone*, but on every street in every city just like this one."

Caro shook his head. The heat was getting to him. He hoped like hell Rod Serling wasn't standing over there talking like that. This situation was strange enough as it was.

He rang the bell as the guy with the paint gun moved around to the far side of the house. How was it even possible to paint in heat like this?

A young, smiling woman answered the door and a man in a golf shirt and blue slacks appeared a moment later behind her.

She looked to be thirty and had on a blue summer dress that accented her clearly athletic body. Her long blonde hair was pulled back and tied and she had a smile that lit up the area around her.

Her husband looked more like a golf professional than anything else, with a short-sleeved Izod shirt and blue slacks. He had close-chopped brown hair and also a smile on his face.

Both had good tans and looked like models out of a sports magazine.

"Yes?" she said.

Caro stuck out his hand and gave his full name, then handed them his business card.

"Come on in out of the heat and the paint fumes," she said and held the door open for him.

He stepped inside and was hit with a shift in temperature of at least thirty degrees. It felt heavenly and made him break out into an instant sweat.

"Thank you," he said, sighing as she closed the door behind him. "I'm from Oregon. Just not used to this heat."

The entry way showed a clean home with a living room of modern and expensive furniture, all tastefully organized.

Through the windows, Caro could see the back yard was as well taken care of as the front.

These people had clearly lived her for a long time. A very long time.

The husband stuck out his hand. "Ben Davis. This is my wife, Stephanie. What can we do for you, Mr. Rosefield?"

Suddenly Caro knew what was happening. Ben and Stephanie Davis had been the names on the property before First Equity foreclosed. More than likely these fine people had been paying their mortgage all along and the payments had gone into some scam or another.

This was worse than he thought. These people were about to have one of the worst days of their entire life. And he was the one who had to deliver the message.

"I'm afraid I don't know how to even approach this," Caro said.

"It's about the house, isn't it?" Stephanie said, smiling, not looking worried in the slightest. "Come on into the kitchen and we'll talk and I'll get us some lemonade."

Caro nodded, feeling even more puzzled then he had before. Maybe Rod Serling really had been standing out there on the driveway.

"I'd love that," he said and followed them into the kitchen that looked like it had been remodeled recently with new granite counters and state-of-the-art appliances.

One area had a counter surrounded by stools with a large bowl of fruit in the center of the countertop.

"Nice," he said, indicating the kitchen as Stephanie

poured him a large glass of lemonade out of a pitcher and Ben sat on a counter stool.

"It's amazing how much work you can do on a house," Ben said, smiling, "when you don't have to pay mortgage payments every month."

Caro stared at Ben. "Then you know why I'm here?"

"Oh, sure, about the house," Stephanie said, still smiling. She sat down on another bar stool and slid her husband a large glass of ice water and cradled a second in her hands.

"Sit, enjoy your drink. We can talk about it," Ben said. "We've worked with banks before. In fact, I worked at Idaho's largest bank before I was laid off three years ago. I know how the system works."

"Yeah, you're here to get the house into shape to be sold," Stephanie said. "Right?"

Caro stared at her and then at her husband while nodding. Usually someone about to be kicked out of their home would be angry. These two just seemed pleased that he was here like they never had guests. He had to be careful about what he said. These two were clearly nuts.

Caro sat on the offered bar stool and took a deep sip from his lemonade. It tasted wonderful. The perfect drink for this kind of hot day.

"So tell me?" he asked, taking another sip and then putting the glass down on the counter. "Why aren't you two upset that your home is about to be sold out from under you?"

"Oh, it's not going to be," Ben said, smiling. Then he

turned to Stephanie. "Which house on the street do you think we should have cleaned up and sold next?"

"Oh, the Benson's old place of course," Stephanie said. "That garage door damage just isn't doing the look of the neighborhood any good at all."

Caro just stared at her. He was right. She *was* nuts, completely nuts.

Ben turned to Caro. "You saw the house two doors down?"

Caro nodded. "Sure I did, but that's not the address on my paperwork. This is the address."

"Oh, I know that," Ben said. "But that's the place you are going to have your clean-up crews go and fix up and paint and let your company sell. Stephanie can even help them pick out colors, can't you dear?" Ben said.

"I'm really good at colors," Stephanie said, nodding and smiling.

"And why would I do that?" Caro asked, now starting to worry that these two might really be dangerous.

"You got a mortgage, Mr. Rosefield?"

"I do," he said.

"And when you saw us in this wonderful home, even doing painting, what did you think?"

"That there had been a massive screw-up somewhere."

"Exactly," Ben said, still smiling like he had just won the lottery. "You thought we had been paying our mortgage regularly for years and some bank somewhere had taken advantage of us. Right?"

"I did," Caro said. "Is that the case?"

"Of course not," Ben said, laughing. "We haven't paid a cent of mortgage for over three years now, and have no intention of ever paying again. In truth, we own this house completely."

"We're just trying to get the rest of the homes along Bryant Street cleaned up," Stephanie said. "We want to get some new neighbors, get things back to normal on our little street of dreams."

Caro wanted to call it more like a street of nightmares and nut-balls, but he didn't say anything. The lawyers were going to have a field day with this one.

"And you and your company would really help out if you would clean up that mess two doors down," Ben said.

Caro just shook his head. "I don't think you understand completely. I'm here for *this* house."

"Oh, we understand completely," Ben said. "But let me show you something. Remember, I worked for a major bank in their mortgage funding area for ten years. I know how all this works."

He climbed off the bar stool and indicated Caro should follow him.

Caro wasn't sure if he should or make a bolt for the front door, but decided he needed to understand just what these people thought they could do to stay mortgage free here. That way he could let his company lawyers know the scam these two crazies were trying to pull.

THREE

Ben led him through the entry way and off the living room into a large side office with a huge computer system with at least five large monitors.

"Ben makes us a lot of money here trading stocks," Stephanie said, smiling.

"I could teach you," Ben said to Caro. "If down the road you are interested in getting out of your job."

"Thanks," Caro said. "But show me why you are not concerned about why I am here."

"Glad to," Ben said, sitting down in a high-backed chair and indicating Caro should come around and stand beside him to watch.

"Sweetie," Ben said to Stephanie, "would you make sure of the address on the old Benson place?"

"Glad to," Stephanie said and turned and headed out the front door as Ben clicked his computer screens out of sleep mode.

On the screen was all the paperwork Caro had for this property and his trip here. Every bit of it, including the house paperwork, his flight times, rental car agreement.

Everything.

"We knew you were coming," Ben said, smiling. "It's why Stephanie made lemonade and we have steaks for the grill with corn and a salad if you want to stay for dinner."

Caro just opened his mouth, but couldn't think of a thing to say, so he just closed it again and just kept staring at the paperwork on the main screen. More than anything now he wanted to run for the front door and maybe the closest police station, but his feet stayed planted beside Ben's chair.

Ben pulled up all the paperwork and history for his house on a second screen and pointed to it. "You see, your company bought this a year ago, but the reality is that the people they bought this house from didn't actually own it either."

Ben pointed at another area of the screen. "I changed that and put this house into the pool for your company so we could get you here today. We didn't know it would be you, of course. But someone from your company would come knocking on the door eventually. It took almost seven months, pretty fast these days."

"You put your own house in a foreclosure auction?" Caro asked, stunned. This guy really, really, really was crazy.

"Oh, sure," Ben said, his fingers dancing over the keys. "Actually, this property is owned by three other companies like yours as well. As I said, we're just trying to get the neighborhood cleaned up."

On one side screen the address and property description of 2761 Bryant Street showed that it was on three other fore-closure sales and notices.

"How can you do that?" Caro asked, his voice choking. "How is that even possible?"

Ben laughed. "As I said, I worked in this area of banking for a decade. I was their computer tech, so they figured I wasn't needed when they downsized. It is stunningly easy in this mess of foreclosures to shift properties around."

"And the state records and recording?"

Ben laughed even harder and pulled up the state records showing that the home Caro was in was actually owned by four different companies and also Ben and Stephanie Davis. It showed Ben and Stephanie as not having a lien on the property at all.

Caro leaned against the chair. "This is crazy," he said. "You are crazy."

"Not really," Ben said. "Just call us the neighborhood clean-up committee and we have drafted your help. I could buy the homes myself and fix them up, but to be honest, I'm having more fun getting companies like your employers to do it for me."

At that moment Stephanie came back in the front door. "Wow, it's hot out there. We need to send the painters home."

"Address first," Ben shouted to her.

"Twenty-seven-thirty-seven," she said and then went back outside and closed the door.

Ben typed in the address and brought up all the paperwork for the property. It showed the property had been sold to First Trust and Loan two months ago.

"Time for a little trading around."

As Caro watched, his mind trying to grasp what he was seeing, Ben's fingers flew over his keyboard and within ten minutes Caro's company owned that property and it was the address on the work order he had. Caro's company had exchanged an equal value property to First Trust in a small town outside of Boise.

And Ben and Stephanie's house was no longer Caro's problem. The lien his company thought they had on it vanished as quickly as a few keystrokes, along with all the filing paperwork, purchase agreements, and state filings.

Caro stood up straight and tried to take a deep breath to clear his head. It almost worked. "I think you just broke about fifty laws."

"More like a hundred," Ben said, smiling. "But there is no way of tracing any of it and trust me, in this world, who is going to care that a few properties got switched around?"

"I'm sure someone can trace it if they wanted," Caro said.

Ben chuckled. "The banks these days can't even find the paperwork on a large percentage of the homes they actually do own. You know that."

Caro didn't want to nod, but he did. Ben was right. Mortgage paperwork was a mess in the best of times.

"So you made up the lien on this property out of whole cloth?" Caro asked.

"I sure did," Ben said. "We had this place paid off five years ago."

"And just to get my company here in your neighborhood to clean up other properties to make your street nicer?"

"You got it," Ben said, smiling. "We got a guy showing up here in a week from a savings and loan out of Utah. But since you made it first, you get the worst of the houses along the street. Trust me, the Bensons didn't go easily when they left."

"So what makes you think I'll go along with you?" Caro asked.

"For a start, you have no evidence of anything different," Ben said.

"Except for the original paperwork in my car," Caro said. "And the files back in my home office."

"I already printed off all the new work orders for you with the new address and Stephanie replaced them in your car while you were in here." Ben pointed at the screen. "I've changed all your companies' official records. They think they own the house down the street and that's where you should be going."

"You've thought of everything except how to keep me quiet," Caro said, now feeling more annoyed than anything else.

Ben hit a key and on one of the previously dark screens an image of Caro's home in Portland came up.

"That's a nice place," Ben said.

"You wouldn't?" Caro asked, stunned.

"I wouldn't want to," Ben said. "Honestly, I wouldn't. And I wouldn't except as a last resort. But you've seen what I can do. I would rather have your help with making our street beautiful again."

Caro knew exactly what the man could do. All the years of making those payments could vanish in a few keystrokes. Caro would spend years trying to dig himself out of a mess that Ben could create in two minutes.

Caro had heard of it happening to other poor souls and he had no desire to be one of them.

And no one would believe his story of a mad hacker putting his own home in foreclosure to help clean up his neighborhood. That was just too crazy to even try to explain.

Ben shut off his computers and stood, pushing Caro back toward the kitchen. "Come on, let me get you something more to drink and we can sit and talk and Stephanie can work on that salad after she sends the painters on their way. After that I can put on the steaks."

Caro took another long drink from the cool lemonade. Then he dropped onto the stool and looked at Ben who had returned to his stool and was smiling.

"You really are crazy," Caro said.

Ben shrugged. "One person's craziness is another's sanity. You can't tell me you think this banking and home mortgage mess is sane. I'm just trying to clean it up a little."

"None of this makes any sense," Caro said. "Not one bit of it. You could have changed the work orders before I got here, sent me to that other house first."

Now Ben was really smiling and nodding as Stephanie came in and joined them. "I could have. You are right."

He looked at Stephanie and smiled. "He figured it out."

"I knew he would," Stephanie said, going to the sink and washing her hands.

"So why didn't you?" Caro asked.

Stephanie poured herself a glass of lemonade and put the pitcher back into the fridge.

"You want to tell him," Ben said to her.

"Because of your daughters," she said. "They need their father to be home."

Caro stood, pushing the stool back, panic ramping up and his heart pounding. "What do you know about my daughters?"

Ben for the first time looked series. "I needed to know as much as I can about a man I'm going to offer a job to."

"You hate this travel," Stephanie said, moving over with the glass of lemonade and sitting down on a stool next to Caro. "Your daughters and your wife hate having you travel so much. It's all over your oldest daughter's Facebook page and in the e-mails your wife sends to her parents and to you when you are traveling."

"You can get to all of that?" Caro asked, his head spinning.

"You would be surprised what Ben can do," Stephanie said, smiling at her husband.

"Not any more I wouldn't," Caro said.

"So I've been planning on getting into real estate in the Portland area," Ben said, "and I need someone who knows houses, knows the area, to run my Oregon branch."

"You get to stay home with your children," Stephanie said.

"I'll pay off your home as a signing bonus and double your salary," Ben said.

"And if I don't agree?" Caro asked.

"We have corn, steaks, salad, and you go back to work tomorrow on that house two doors down. It's just an offer, nothing more."

"Actually," Stephanie said, "we'd like you to get that fixed up before you quit your current job."

"And why would I quit one job to do the same job with you?" Caro asked, trying to keep the anger out of his voice.

"It wouldn't be exactly the same job," Ben said, smiling.

"So what exactly would it be?"

At this point Caro was convinced, completely convinced, that he was facing two of the crazier people he had ever had the misfortune to run into. And every part of his brain said he needed to get out of that house quickly.

Stephanie was beaming and Ben's smile couldn't get any bigger.

Two fruitcakes. They were both nuts. Caro stood and backed a step away from the counter. Now even with air-conditioning he was sweating.

"This was Stephanie's idea," Ben said.

"I thought if it after we watched the Bensons get evicted," she said. "We liked them."

Ben nodded. "Yeah, good people. So I decided I could use the money we have, plus some money from the banks that I can get access to, to work to keep people in their homes."

"He's made a lot of money in stocks," she said, smiling.

Ben laughed. "I'm good at shorting bank stocks at exactly the right time."

"So we want you to meet with families who are about to be evicted," Stephanie said.

"I'll buy up their mortgage if you say they are solid people," Ben said. "You figure out what they can really afford and we'll set that up for them to pay. Make sure they stay in their home and the bank doesn't make a profit from their hardship."

"Can I think about it?" Caro asked, taking another step back. These two weren't just nuts, they were living in a fairy tale land.

"Of course," Ben said. "Take all the time you like. The job is yours if you want it."

"Thanks," he said, and turned for the door.

The heat hit him in the face like a slap and he made it to his car and got it started as fast as he could, getting the air-conditioning running. On the seat where he had left them was the paperwork he had brought from Oregon, but now the address was two doors down the street.

An address he never would have questioned an hour before.

FOUR

He headed the big rental up Bryant Street until he found a shady place to park out of sight of good old Ben and Stephanie.

Then leaving the car running, he grabbed up his cell phone and hit speed dial. Denise at the home office in Portland answered. She was one of the best there was at computers and tracking housing paperwork. If anyone on the planet could find records that had been tampered with, it was Denise.

"I need you to pull up some paperwork on a house

here," Caro said. "I want to make sure everything is in order before I move one more step on it."

"Smart thinking," Denise said. "You never know in these days."

"You got that right," Caro said.

Over the next thirty minutes, with the air-conditioning blowing on his face, he had her search every record the company had on the house on Bryant Street in Boise, Idaho.

No sign of tampering, no sign of anything different. The address he needed to work on was the empty house with the damaged garage door. The company had bought it eight months before at auction.

"Looks all square to me," Denise said finally. "State filing is all confirmed as well. We own it all fair and square."

He thanked her and hung up, then sat staring down Bryant Street.

Ben had been for real, or the entire thing had been an ugly heat vision. Or Caro really had fallen into the *Twilight Zone.*

Right now he needed to believe that Ben and Stephanie were for real. That they were two people with more money and skills than sense who just wanted to help people.

He hit speed dial again on his phone and this time got his wife.

"Wow, this is a pleasant surprise," Mary said.

"Where are you at?"

"Picking up Cindie," she said. "I got ten minutes before

she gets out of school. Something wrong? You sound stressed."

"Sort of am," Caro said.

Then, as he had done with everything since they met, he told her what had happened with Ben and Stephanie.

"They want to save people's homes for them?" she asked after he had finished giving her the story, job offer and all. Everything but the threat against their house.

After working with Denise in his home office, Caro was convinced Ben would never do that unless really, really pushed. He didn't need to. He could cover his tracks completely and make anything Caro said look like a nut job talking. So Mary didn't need to worry about that happening. Caro had no thoughts of pushing.

"It sure seems that way," Caro said.

"He's really that good on computers, huh?"

"He's the best I have ever seen," Caro said.

"And you would be at home and getting twice your salary?" she asked.

He could hear the excitement in her voice. He had no doubt which way she was going to go.

And now that he had stopped and thought about it and proved to himself that Ben could do what he seemed to appear to do, Caro was starting to like the idea more and more.

"It seems that way," Caro said. "It would be nice to be home with you and the girls every night."

"It would be wonderful," Mary said, her voice almost

breathless as she said that. "But can these two afford to do what they are saying they want to do?"

"I have a hunch that Ben can do pretty much what he wants," Caro said. "But I will check to make sure."

At that moment in the background his daughter Cindie climbed into the car and Mary said high and told her to get buckled in.

Caro looked down the hot neighborhood street and wished beyond anything that he was there with them.

Sometimes guy has to take a chance when given to him, no matter how crazy that chance was.

"Mary," he said. "I think I'm going to go back and talk with them again."

"Oh, that would be so wonderful if this worked out," she said. "Good luck. Say goodbye to daddy."

Cindie said in the background, "Bye, Daddy. Hurry home."

And with that Mary hung up.

Caro was again alone in the air-conditioning of his rented car sitting on a hot street in a town he never wanted to visit again.

FIVE

He sat thinking for another five minutes, running every-thing through his mind, then headed back toward Ben and Stephanie's home.

He stood in the heat once again and rang their bell.

And again both of them answered with wide smiles and

invited him in and got him seated in their kitchen with a wonderful-tasting glass of lemonade in his hands.

"I talked to my wife and did some research on just how good you are at changing the paperwork."

"He's good, isn't he?" Stephanie said.

"Very good," Caro said. "My company has one of the best computer people I know and she couldn't find a thing wrong with your paperwork on the Benson house up the street."

Ben only nodded.

"But if I did agree to work for you, I would need a few assurances."

"Go on," Ben said.

"I'll need to know you have the money to do all of this," Caro said.

"Fair enough," Ben said. "Stephanie, do you mind if I show Mr. Rosefield our accounts later?"

"Not at all," Stephanie said. "It's a logical request since he has a family to protect."

"And you'll do this all above board?" Caro asked. "Last thing my daughters would need would be to have their father sent to jail."

"Ninety-nine percent of the time," Ben said. "But I have to be honest with you, I'm not going to feel bad helping a bank help a family stay in their home. And that might take a little computer hacking, but no theft. That much I can promise."

"No theft, ever?"

"Ever," Ben said. "I couldn't sleep if I did. Like cheating on my taxes. Not worth losing the sleep."

"And if he did I'd make him pay for it as well," Stephanie said, smiling.

"And she would, too," Ben said. "It's why I did the property trade so your company would be out no money and neither would the owner of the Benson place."

Caro nodded. He could live with a little computer hacking for the right cause.

They talked for another thirty minutes and Ben and Stephanie filled in all his questions better than he had hoped, actually.

He was convinced they were crazy. Crazy to even try something this stupid. But he was starting to like their kind of crazy and for the first time in years he felt excited about the coming work he would be doing.

Finally, he had one more question. "You have a guy coming from Utah next week to do the same thing there?"

"We hope so," Stephanie said. "Someone has to do this."

"So all this was nothing more than a giant job interview, right?"

"Basically," Ben said, smiling. "It's going to take a certain type of person to do what we are hoping to do. So we need to run each of you through this to see how each of you react."

"And I passed?" Caro asked. "You're still offering me the job?"

"It is yours," Ben said, extending his hand

"You know, you both are crazy," Caro said, shaking

Ben's hand and smiling for the first time in the day. "But I guess I am as well."

"Let's hope you are the first of many crazies to come," Ben said.

"This is the *Twilight Zone*, right?" Caro asked. "Rod Serling is standing in the corner, smoking, talking about how sometimes it takes ordinary people to help out other ordinary people."

Stephanie and Ben both laughed.

"Nope," Stephanie said. "This is Bryant Street, a street like every other street in the country, where good families live and magic can sometimes happen."

Caro raised his glass of lemonade in a toast. "Rod Serling himself could not have said it better."

Dean Wesley Smith

USA Today Bestselling Writer

A Funny Look
at Love, Death,
and the Movies

The Yellow of the Flickering Past

THE YELLOW OF THE FLICKERING PAST

He killed her with a magic spell, buried her in the basement, and now she nags him every day to take her to the movies.

Just as she nagged him when she lived.

The woman never got tired of buttered popcorn and a dark theater.

A really strange Bryant Street ghost story about love, death, and the movies.

ACT ONE: A YELLOW OIL MESS

Sixteen days after I killed her, I took my dead wife to a movie.

She had always loved movies.

Actually I think she loved the memory of movies more than any one film. And she loved the smell of the buttered popcorn you could buy in theaters, even if the butter was actually only a melted yellow oil from big yellow cans. She said it was part of the movie- going experience and that was all that mattered.

On our first date to a movie I laughed when she asked for an "extra large, extra butter, please."

"You know that shit will kill you?" I said as the guy with a thousand pimples pumped the handle of the butter machine like he was huddled over his first Playboy center-fold. Miss July.

"Sure," my date, soon-to-be wife, later-to-be-dead wife, had said. She never once offered me any of her popcorn. That was sort of how we argued from then on.

And we argued a lot.

She asked for the same "Extra large, extra butter" every time we went to a movie. She never missed a movie.

We went to a lot of movies.

Of course, people who saw us at the movies thought we made the perfect couple. "Fit together," they would say, but after I came out of the coma induced by new love and the first year of marriage, I just didn't see why. She was a light blonde, with a large, white-toothed smile, and wide, inno-cent green eyes. I actually had light brown hair, but I suppose it looked closer to her color because I kept it cut so short. I had dark brown eyes and people said I squinted a lot. I was almost five-six when I wore my good shoes, and even in heels she still wasn't as tall as I was.

Besides that, we argued all the time and I hated movies and didn't eat popcorn, especially with yellow oil.

The last year of our marriage I started daydreaming about the dreaded yellow oil. I figured no human body could digest that stuff, so it must have been building up in her body over the five years and seven days we were together. Maybe even for years before, just waiting for the right circumstances to set it all off in a huge bang. I dreamed she would explode and the police would just nod and say, "Yup. Yellow oil build-up."

But I could never figure out how to set off the explosion. I watched the papers for months hoping to read about another yellow oil explosion, but never did.

I even consented to sex one night that last year, thinking that might set her off. But the thought of her exploding had me so excited that she said I didn't last long enough to even get her hot. Maybe that was why it didn't work.

Sadly, she never did explode, or even melt. The yellow oil didn't kill her.

I did that. I killed her with a curse from a book of Wizard curses I bought at a used bookstore downtown. A big brown book with a guy on the cover wearing a pointed hat and a star-covered robe.

I wish the yellow oil had killed her instead, in a huge, messy wife-explosion. I wouldn't have minded cleaning up the mess.

After my now-dead wife would get her "extra large, extra butter," she used to love the walk down the carpeted halls of the multiplex theater, past the posters of the other movies showing in all the other theaters. She would stop and point out every show she wanted to see, as if I really cared. The last few years I even stopped pretending I did care, but she kept right on pointing them out.

Then, after the pointing-at-the-poster routine was done she would go into the theater and look around in the low light to find just the right, perfect seat. Finding the exact right seat was always treated as one of the most important events in life. I think a good seat meant more to her than Christmas or her mother's birthday.

Once she had found that perfect place, she always whispered to me that she hoped no one would sit in front of her.

I always just nodded and she would settle in, happy, content, wide eyes focused on the blank screen ahead.

On the times when someone did have the nerve to take the seat in front of her, she would make a rude, almost pig-like noise and make us move to new, perfect seats. Which, of course, again took time. And once settled she would again whisper to me that she hoped no one would sit in front of her.

For a popular movie we moved a lot and usually ended up sitting down front. Then I would get a sore neck from looking straight up at the screen. I always felt I was looking up the actor's nose. Nose hair can really distract from the plot of a movie.

I think, more than even the movie, I think my now-dead wife loved the previews of the coming attractions. Something about the possibility of a future trip to the movies held her spellbound like a deer in front of a car's headlights. We never saw a preview of a movie after which she didn't whisper to me that she wanted to see the movie. And didn't it look just wonderful?

The word "wonderful" was always followed by a long sigh. Just once I wish she would have sighed like that after we had sex.

Near the end of the second year of our marriage I started writing letters to the theater begging them, at first, and then demanding, that they not show previews of coming movies. A nasty phone call from the police department made me stop writing.

The theater kept playing the coming attractions.

She kept wanting to see every movie.

Of course, we went to them all.

And they all had coming attractions.

I still get dizzy just thinking about it.

That, and all that yellow oil she ate.

Act Two: The Unlawful Christmas Argument

The idea to take my dead wife to a movie was hers, of course. It seemed that my killing her, then wrapping her body in plastic and stuffing it in an old trunk in the basement didn't even slow down her love for movies. I guess I was wrong to expect that it would.

For over two weeks after I killed her I kept saying no. No way in hell was I going to be seen in a movie theater with the ghost of my dead wife. And there were no curses or formulas in my Wizard's book for getting rid of ghosts, so I had to keep listening to her and arguing with her.

And of course, as when we were married, she ended up winning all the arguments. She finally used the old "it's-almost-Christmas" routine and I caved in like a tunnel cut through mud. But I said I would do it on my conditions.

She didn't care about that. But she did say we had to follow the ghost rules. Wizard curses, ghost rules, my conditions. This was going to be a very complicated trip to the movies.

Before I bought the Wizard's book, I didn't know Wizards even existed. And I never expected that I might be one, but since one of the Wizard curses worked for me, I suppose I am. But so far I've not been able to make another curse work. But I'm going to keep practicing, because what Wizards can do is really cool stuff.

Before she died I didn't realize that ghosts had rules, either. But they do. A lot of them. And I discovered the ghost rules are sometimes a little tricky to figure out. For example, there was the main rule about why she was still even around. She said she had her reasons and they were for her to know and me to find out. She said that a lot during our marriage and I never found out a thing.

I didn't expect that now that she was a ghost this time was going to be any different.

As far as going to a movie went, she figured that if I could get her body close enough to the theater, she, her ghost, not her body, could go inside with me and see the movie. For some ghost rule or another she had to stay fairly close to her body, which is why she had been hanging around the house.

She decided I could put her body in the car and then park the car next to the theater. A simple plan, really. Just get a two-plus week-old dead body right up next to a public theater and then leave it for two hours. I laughed at her when she said that was what we needed to do. I flat out said no way.

She kept at me, kept me up all night again with the what-a-wonderful-Christmas-present it would be for her. I tried a Wizard curse on her that was supposed to have turned her into a frog, but she stayed a ghost and kept at me.

I gave in again. About sunrise. Using Christmas in arguments should be outlawed in all marriages, even after death.

We waited until after dark, which really didn't upset her because she hated the cheap, early shows. She always said going to a regular show was much better. I never did figure out what was the difference between a cheap show and a regular show, except the price. Every time I asked her about the difference she just looked at me as if I was stupid and just couldn't see.

At least this time I would only have to buy one ticket.

As I loaded her body into the hatchback, she stood in the driveway to watch for the neighbors and cars on the street. It had only been a few weeks since she had died and the decay and smell wasn't too bad. Or at least I tried to convince myself that it wasn't that bad.

I had her wrapped in three sheets of plastic and taped so tightly shut no air, or anything else for that matter, could get in there. Yet I was sure as I draped her over my shoulder that I could smell a rotten, nose-clogging aroma of decay. Like a dead dog three days beside the road.

She laughed when I mentioned it and told me it was my guilt catching up with me. But I swore I could smell her rotting, right through the plastic bags and all the tape, guilt or no guilt.

It took what seemed like an eternity to get her body settled and the hatch closed. The backs of newer cars just weren't made for holding bodies like the trunks of the cars my parents owned. Those trunks were big. To get her in the Impala hatchback I had to remove the spare. No telling what problems we would have if we had a flat.

She came through the door without opening it and settled into the passenger seat.

"This is going to be so much fun," she said, and I shuddered. She had said those very words before every movie we ever went to, almost like a recording.

Maybe this was my hell. No maybe about it. I was in hell. I was destined to take my dead wife to a movie three times a week for the rest of my life. Maybe I should just kill myself now and get it over with.

If I could only be certain that would end it.

ACT THREE: A YELLOW TINGE

"You won't think it's sweet if we get caught," I said

about halfway to the theater after she told me I was being sweet for taking her to a movie. "I get tossed in jail for killing you, and you'll end up haunting the local cemetery."

She shrugged. "Couldn't be much worse than hanging around here with you."

"Now don't start," I said. "This is how you got killed in the first place.

"Don't you dare blame me again for what happened." She had her hands on her hips, the sign she was getting mad. "I'm the one who is dead, remember."

"How can I ever forget?"

Actually, I had never really totally hated her. At least not enough yet to kill her. But I suppose it was building to that. I sure had wished she was dead enough times.

It was her way of arguing that got to me. One afternoon she started in on me. Or, as she tells it, I started in on her. Either way doesn't make much difference. I got so mad I yelled a Wizard curse at her that I had just read that morning. She laughed, so for a special effect I tossed a handful of sparkle dust from the magic shop in her face. I read that Wizards were always using sparkle dust and I guess it worked.

She backed up away from me rubbing her eyes, tripped, and hit her head hard on the edge of the counter as she went down.

I was over her immediately. I didn't like the way her head hitting that counter had sounded. A sick, deep smacking and cracking sound. Granted, I had cursed her dead, but I wasn't sure I really wanted her that way.

Too late. She was already dead. And her ghost was standing above me leaning over her own body.

"Now see what you have done," she had said. Even dead she had started out annoying.

We rode the rest of the way in silence to the theater. I remembered we had done that a lot. Especially the year before she died. Actually, in the two weeks since she died we had gotten along better than ever before. Something about her not expecting sex, I think.

I parked as close as I could to the multiplex theater building and suddenly she was in a good mood again. She clapped her hands together and floated out of the car before I even had it stopped.

"I'm in heaven," she said, moving toward the ticket window.

I shook my head, muttering that she was a long way from heaven, but I certainly wished she would go there soon. I locked the car and checked twice to see if the hatch was shut tight and the blanket over her body was in place.

By the time I had bought my ticket to the show she wanted to see, she was already inside, floating in front of the popcorn counter, looking sad.

I moved up beside her and as softly as I could, without moving my lips, I asked, "What's wrong?"

She pointed at the popcorn.

"You knew you wouldn't be able to eat any?" I whispered.

She shook her head. "No, it's not that. I can pick it up and put it in my mouth." To demonstrate she took a piece from the counter and popped it into her mouth and chewed with her mouth half open. Thank god no one was watching.

"So what's the problem? And since when can you pick up stuff?"

She shrugged. "I've been doing that for days now. But I can't taste the popcorn."

More stupid ghost rules.

I stared at her for a moment and then glanced around the theater lobby to see if anyone was watching. Again we were in luck.

"Maybe I can find a Wizard spell to help you," I said. "Or maybe you'll just get better with practice." I regretted saying that immediately.

"Oh, you think so? Then get an extra large, extra butter. I'll practice all the way through the movie."

I was about to object when this couple moved up behind me and I was forced to get the guy behind the counter's attention and buy an extra large, extra butter popcorn and a small drink.

By the time I found her in the sixth theater down the hall the previews were already starting. I started to say something and she shushed me, just like she used to do when she was alive.

Dead. Alive. Nothing changes.

I balanced the popcorn on the rail between us and she began to eat handfuls, dropping exactly the same amount that she used to do when she was alive, only this time the dropped popcorn went through her and gathered in a pile on the seat. I'd have to ask her later how that worked and why I couldn't see the popcorn after it was inside her. More and more strange ghost rules.

I glanced around to see if anyone was watching or sitting close. We were in luck. This movie was a real dog and there were only five other people in the theater.

After every preview she leaned over and whispered that she wanted to see that movie, just like she had always done. And, as when she was alive, the thought made me shudder, but now for different reasons.

I spent most of the movie trying to work out plans of escape. I even thought of just going out of the theater and walking away. But I didn't have the guts to do that. Besides, eventually the police would find the car and her body and I would get caught. The life of a fugitive just wasn't one for me.

When the movie ended she sighed. "I really love movies."

"No kidding," I said under my breath and luckily she ignored me. I sat still, watching the credits and waiting until the other people left before standing.

"Too bad you couldn't just stay here."

Again she sighed. "That would be wonderful."

We headed out the back door near the screen in silence and it wasn't until I was at the car that I had realized what I had seen.

The multiplex theater's back door was right beside the screen. Under the screen, like in old theaters, was a stage, only this stage was fake, just used to get the screen up in the air. A maintenance man, or someone, must have left the access door open to the area under the stage, revealing rough planking on the floor spaced evenly over hard packed dirt.

There was nothing else under there and no reason for anyone to ever go under there.

"You really want to stay here?" I asked as she settled into her seat.

She looked at me with that questioning look, meaning she didn't understand. I always had liked that look because it meant she didn't understand something about me. She always took such pride in knowing everything about me, so that look had always cheered me up and tonight was no exception.

I pointed back at the closed door. "Go back through there and take a look under the stage."

"But—"

"Just do it." I loved having the upper hand.

She shrugged and floated/walked/moved toward the closed metal theater door and then through it like it was the surface of a lake.

A full minute later she was back, excited. "I see what you are thinking. You could bury my body under the stage and I could see all the movies I wanted."

I nodded and she tried to hug me, which failed totally. But I suppose it was the thought that counted.

We went home, got my gloves and a shovel, and I tossed in my Wizards book just in case I might need it. We were back to the theater in less than an hour. I backed the car right up to the closest place I could get near the stage door and we waited until the next show ended and the people were leaving.

She went inside and stood guard and when she motioned that the coast was clear, I blocked the door open. As the credits were playing I got her body from the car and under the stage.

While she watched the movie again with eight live people, I buried her. I had to be real quiet, especially taking out and replacing the flooring planks. But I got it done, finishing the digging during the noisy love scene in the middle and then putting back the flooring during the loud chase scene at the end.

I did a quick Wizard invisibility blessing over her grave, then left the shovel in the back corner, as if it had been left by a workman. I went out behind the last movie-goer of the last show.

She met me in the car, smiling. "Thanks," she said.

I think that was the first time in years she had said that to me. I was taken aback. "My pleasure," was all I could think to say.

"Would you come tomorrow night and see a movie with me?"

"Sure," I said.

She clapped her hands together like a kid. "Great. You can buy me some popcorn."

"I'd be glad to," I said. And I really meant it. Since then I went to the movies there about once a week. No one ever talked about the ghost of the twelve-plex theater, except to complain about rude noises from empty seats behind them.

No one ever found her body.

I bought her popcorn every week and we never fought again. She seemed totally contented.

But after a few years I noticed she had this yellow tinge about her. I tried a Wizard curse to help her, but it did no good. I figured it was just too much yellow oil build-up.

Smith's STORIES

DEAN WESLEY SMITH

A LACK OF TOMORROW

A Bryant Street Story

A LACK OF TOMORROW

Rose Brackhahn just lost her dear husband, but somehow managed to do the best she could in her wonderful home on Bryant Street.

Then the world decided to kill itself, so Rose prepared to keep going, as she knew her husband would have wanted her to.

But not all things are possible, even on Bryant Street.

———

On the day the human race decided to start over, Rose Brackhahn spent until almost dark working in her vegetable garden in the backyard of her home on Bryant Street. The garden only took up about a quarter of the yard, but it felt huge to Rose's seventy-two years of a bad back and a tweaked knee. Yet she managed to keep it producing into the fall every year. She loved the fresh tomatoes, strawberries, and zucchini best of everything she grew.

It had been a warm day, but not hot. Rose wore what she called her "get dirty" clothes of jeans, a really old spaghetti-stained cotton blouse, and tennis shoes that had seen better days twenty years before. She had her regular "kick around the house" clothes waiting for her on her back porch to change into when she was done. Jeans, a cotton blouse, and nicer tennis shoes.

Rose hadn't worn a dress in maybe twenty years, since her husband Lenny had been killed in a work accident. Couldn't see much point to it. But her good ones still hung in her closet and every few years she sent them off to be cleaned just so they would always be ready if she had to wear one.

Lenny had been a handsome man in his own way. Broad shoulders from working construction and a smile that had melted her when they first met.

He was taller than her and she loved to tuck right in under his arm so he could hold her. She had brown hair like his and both of them had green eyes, which always got them comments when they went out.

He had been a gentle man and she missed him every day, talked to him at times with decisions, and dreamed about him at night, good dreams, with him smiling and them dancing.

Lenny would be proud of her garden this year, but now, her back was telling her she was done for the day, at least in the garden. She still needed to cook herself a nice dinner and there was *Jeopardy!* to watch before bed. She and Lenny loved that show and after he had died she had just continued watching it, sometimes pretending he was beside her.

She had just finished changing her clothes and washing her hands and arms when the first alert siren went off.

"Now what?" she asked out loud. The damn sirens went off far too often in this town. She remembered back when the emergency alert sirens only went off if something really serious was happening.

She went to the television and clicked it on, only to discover that something really, really serious was happening.

It seemed that Russia, about to collapse from all the sanctions imposed on it, decided the United States and Europe were to blame and managed to launch a lot of nuclear bombs. Basically Russia decided to kill itself and take the human race with it.

United States and European allies had launched a lot of rockets in return.

North Korea, taking advantage of the moment to kill itself as well, had launched a bunch of rockets at the United States. The United States and its allies were in the process of taking off the map the country formally known as North Korea.

Russia had also launched a bunch of rockets at China, so China was retaliating.

Everything seemed to be aimed at Russia or North

Korea. Even China fired some big rockets at North Korea, their former alley.

Live feeds from around the world were coming in of big mushroom clouds.

"Lenny," Rose said to the room. "Looks like we have finally killed ourselves."

Rose had lived her entire life under the threat that this would happen someday. It seemed like a bad movie that it was happening now.

Rose left the television going and went into her kitchen and cooked herself a nice dinner, maybe one of the best she had had in a long time. A celebration-type dinner with a steak, potatoes, and some fresh asparagus from her garden.

Then she put it on a plate on her kitchen table and went into her bedroom and put on her best dress for the occasion.

If she had gone to a funeral, she would have worn the dress. It seemed appropriate for the funeral of the human race.

Then she poured herself and Lenny a glass of wine from a bottle she had opened for cooking a few days before.

She held her glass up in a toast. "Lenny dear, looks like I will be joining you fairly soon."

She sipped the wine and then turned the television so that she could watch the end of the modern world while she ate dinner at the kitchen table.

Things just kept going, but she still enjoyed the steak and the melted butter over the asparagus was wonderful.

She did the dishes as more and more of the world's cities just vanished right in front of cameras.

Now her home on Bryant Street was on the outskirts of Portland, Oregon, but she doubted anyone would waste a bomb on Portland unless one of the North Korean shots just got lucky.

After an hour more of watching the end of the world instead of *Jeopardy!*, she changed into night clothes and with one last look at the dying world, shut off the television and went to bed, using earplugs to block most of the sounds of the sirens.

The next morning, as usual, the sun through her bedroom window woke her up. She took out the earplugs to hear the morning birds chirping as if nothing had happened yesterday.

Maybe it hadn't, for all she knew. She was an older woman and sometimes just imagined things, like the time she imagined Lenny was beside her in bed and was comforting her.

Of course, that had been caused by a fever and she was doing fine as it was without Lenny, but not a day went by she didn't miss him.

She fixed herself her normal breakfast and then, while eating, turned the television back on.

It seemed she had not been imagining things.

All of Russia was gone, most of Europe, North Korea, and Japan. The East Coast of the United States was pretty much wiped out and there was no sign yet of any of the major leaders in Washington. All were either still in shelters or feared dead.

Southern California, San Francisco, Las Vegas, Phoenix,

and Seattle were gone. As she had figured, Portland, Oregon, and a bunch of Midwest towns had been spared.

A lot of Canada and Mexico and most of the Southern Hemisphere had been spared as well except for cities in Australia and South Africa.

She watched for a bit, then decided before it got too late in the year, she needed to expand her garden. She was going to need it.

So she spent a long day in the garden, expanding it and planting potatoes and more tomatoes.

Then she went inside and spent the early evening doing an inventory of her pantry. Luckily she had many jars of peanut butter and many, many boxes of crackers, one of her favorite snacks. With the veggies from her garden, she could make it a while until things started to rebuild.

She watched the television again as the newscasters tried to make sense of everything that had happened. Rose knew there was no sense to be made of it, but it would have helped if Lenny had been there to talk her through some of it.

So she shut off the television and took her sore body to bed.

Every day she worked in her garden and planned for a winter without heat and things like that, whatever she could think of.

Then on the fifth day there was no sun, just a dark, black cloud and the people on the television warned everyone to stay inside.

So she did. She had all of her blinds down and her

curtains drawn, so she turned on a light over her favorite reading chair and took a book that she had been wanting to read from the shelf of books in her living room and spent the afternoon resting her back and sore knee and just reading.

Turned out to be one of the most pleasant days she had had in a long time.

The next day, as was normal for Portland, Oregon, it rained and the gutters ran black with the soot from the sky. The television said it was dangerous stuff from all the bombs over Russia and China and North Korea.

It rained for two more days and everything outside Rose's windows turned black.

As did her treasured garden.

It was almost as if she could see the plants wither and just die when covered with the black soot from the sky.

It seemed from the television that all of Portland and the rest of the United States was covered in thick, deadly radiation. Unless they were underground, no one would survive.

"Not long now, Lenny," she said. "I'll be joining you."

Civilization and a lot of the human race would die. But the scientists said that there would be survivors and that the human race in a thousand years would rebuild.

Rose just shrugged.

She had, after her husband's sudden death, come to grips with both living alone and dying alone. It was just what she did. Bombs or cancer or a bad heart. She had always known something was going to take her on to the next world.

Too bad the rest of humanity had to go with her.

After two more weeks of keeping herself distracted by reading, Rose really missed the fresh vegetables from her garden, but even with more rain, the clouds never left and everything stayed black.

And it was getting colder at night, but so far the power was still on and newscasters were still at the television station, so she watched them some each day. She figured they were being brave and doing their jobs, so she owed them some of her time, even though they didn't have nice things to say about the future and at times broke down into tears themselves.

She hadn't cried. She was going to see Lenny again.

In another week she was down to eating peanut butter and crackers and not a lot of those. She had no idea why she wanted to stay alive longer, but she knew if she took the easy way out, Lenny would be disappointed in her.

She had opened her blinds during the gray days and had seen no one moving at all outside. Not even any tire tracks in the black mud on the streets.

Where would anyone go?

Covered in black mud and dust, the Bryant Street homes looked more Art Deco than anything. Weird and kind of pretty at the same time.

Two weeks later the black clouds had not lifted. Rose had run out of food two days before and just about the time she ran out of food, the power went out.

Her house, without heat, got amazingly cold very quickly, even though it was the middle of the summer. The people on the television before they quit called this a nuclear winter. Rose didn't remember it being this cold ever, even in the middle of the winter in Portland.

And Rose had developed a number of nasty sores on her arms and legs that the news people said everyone would get from the radiation poisoning.

Rose could feel herself slipping away on the second day without power. She was covered in blankets and shivering and the hunger pains had just about vanished since she had nothing to eat at all in days. Just water, but the glass of water on the table beside her had frozen while she slept.

"Well, it was a fun run," she said to her home, a home she had loved on a street she had loved. "Thanks!"

Then she just pulled the blankets and quilts up tight under her chin and closed her eyes. "Hey, Lenny. Here I come and you had damn well better be ready."

Smith's
STORIES

DEAN WESLEY SMITH

THE MAN WHO
TASTED THE OTHER SIDE
A Bryant Street Story

THE MAN WHO TASTED THE OTHER SIDE

Strange stuff happens when a person dies. Glen Gunderson died of a heart attack in a bank and found himself in a bakery full of the most heavenly goodies.

Then the doctors brought him back to life and things got really, really strange. But since he lived on Bryant Street, that should be expected.

———

Glen Gunderson died last summer.

Heart attack while standing in a line in a bank.

From what he understood later, he had made quite a scene, but two customers had some CPR training and they managed to keep the blood in his body flowing. The hospital was only two blocks away, so they got to him fairly quickly and ended up doing a bypass that afternoon and he recovered.

Glen had never been an unhealthy man, and not that far overweight. He stood about five-eight and had short-cut brown hair. But flat dying on the tile floor of a bank at the age of forty-eight sent a wake-up call to the rest of his life.

Glen lived alone in a small two-bedroom home in a quiet subdivision. He was a confirmed bachelor and never intended to change that. He liked his life and the control over everything he did.

He worked as the CFO of a mid-sized manufacturing firm and loved his job and the people he worked with.

He went out with the group from the office on Friday night for happy hour and had one glass of wine per night at home. He didn't smoke, but he also didn't exercise much at all.

After the time in the hospital, that changed.

He lost weight, joined a gym and actually used the membership, and for most of the time, he ate right.

Most of the time.

Glen on the matter of food had one large issue. The time he was dead had changed his appetite. The dream or the event or whatever had happened to him while he was dead made eating right almost impossible.

Before he died, he could take or leave sweet things. Sure, he enjoyed a rare piece of cherry pie, and liked one piece of pumpkin pie with his restaurant meal on Thanksgiving day.

And at Christmas, at the parties he was invited to, he

liked the cookies more than anything, often taking a few home with him for a snack on Christmas morning.

But when he died, he found himself in the most luscious-smelling bakery. The sweet and rich smell so thick, the air could almost be cut.

Fresh warm breads filled one wall, cinnamon rolls covered in thick white sugar icing filled a case in front of him, and hundreds of platters of cookies and cakes and pies filled cases to his right.

The hospital told him he had only been dead for less than thirty seconds before CPR was started on him. But to him, that thirty seconds had stretched almost a lifetime.

For all he knew it had been a lifetime. He sure didn't pretend to understand what had happened and he still didn't believe in a God, unless that God could make the most amazing cinnamon rolls ever.

In that lifetime Glen lived in those thirty seconds of being dead, Glen just stayed in the bakery and ate. He remembered he had no desire to go anywhere else.

He ate everything, and the tastes were almost orgasmic in nature with every bite. He would tear apart and eat entire loaves of fresh white bread, dipping each piece in hot butter.

Just remembering that made his mouth water.

In one sitting alone he ate an entire case of cinnamon rolls and the last one tasted as good as the first one. Maybe better.

And while he was doing that, in those thirty seconds of death, he gained weight.

Massive amounts of weight as time went on and he kept eating and eating and eating.

Cookies and pies and cakes and breads.

He ate it all and never got full and it always tasted wonderful.

Every bite.

Until finally, one day, he was so large, he could no longer get to his feet to go get himself more pie.

And that was when he returned to life.

But now he had a craving for sweets of any kind. He could go through a family-sized bag of M&Ms in an hour by himself. And then lick out the inside of the bag.

He would buy a pie to take home and eat it instead of dinner.

The fear of dying kept him exercising and most of the time eating right. And because of the fear, he had lost weight and everyone commented on how healthy he looked.

But that didn't make the craving for anything sweet go away.

He had died and gone to bakery heaven and now he wanted more.

But he didn't want to die again to get it.

So he developed a plan.

He got a calorie and step counter, one of those things you hook to your wrist like a watch. And he decided he would exercise off every extra calorie he ate. That way he could have a few sweets or desserts and stay alive.

A fine idea in theory.

And for the first month it worked.

And he got in better and better shape, which allowed him to eat more and more.

He started running on his subdivision street, going out to do a mile, then a few miles.

By the end of the third month he was clocking over eight miles a day running every day, without missing a day. It was easier to run than to control his impulse to eat sweets.

He counted every calorie he ate obsessively and made sure he matched it with calories burned on his counter.

And the more he allowed himself to enjoy the sweet things he remembered when he had died, the more he pushed himself to exercise.

And then one day it happened, his worst nightmare.

He tripped going up a curb and twisted his ankle.

A neighbor saw him and helped him home and he made it on his own to the doctor, who wrapped his ankle and told him to stay off of it for at least a few weeks and no running for at least two months.

Glen got home and immediately tossed out every sweet thing he had in the house. He couldn't trust himself.

He could only eat sweets if he was exercising and now he couldn't exercise, so he could no longer eat what he craved.

Now Glen was a strong man, with a strong will to live.

But the clear memory of that bakery was stronger than Glen, and two days later he had a piece of pie with lunch.

It was a slippery slope from there.

On the way home he bought a box of doughnuts and

tried to make them last. He ate the entire box in thirty minutes.

The next day he got a cinnamon roll on the way to work, had a box of doughnuts at break, ate most of an entire cherry pie at lunch, had two large bags of M&Ms to get him through the afternoon, and dinner consisted of fresh white bread with raspberry jam and a massive amount of strawberry shortcake.

By the time Glen's ankle healed, he knew he was in trouble.

Big, big trouble. His experience of that bakery when he died had changed him. And not for the better and he knew it.

He had gone and gotten professional help because in two months since hurting his ankle, he had gained almost forty pounds.

The professional help got him off the sweets cold turkey, just like stopping smoking. He got back on good food and exercising and had to report what he had done three times a day to his counselor.

Slowly, very slowly, weight came down again.

Three months after admitting he had a problem and getting help, Glen was back at full running weight and hadn't had anything sweet or dessert-like items.

But he had transferred the obsession to the running.

His neighbors would always wave as he went by for his morning seven miles before going to work. He liked that and always waved back. It made him feel good and he smiled and they smiled and all was well with the world.

Then a month later he added in a four-mile run at lunch. That wasn't enough.

A month later, after a quick healthy dinner, he started to clock in another six or seven miles, trying to do just a little more each day.

The neighbors along the street waved at him then as well.

Now a few of his friends were worried about him being too thin, but he assured them it was just running weight.

Six months after starting to run again, he ran his first official marathon and it seemed too easy. So he kept training and signed up for an ultra marathon.

He no longer thought about snacks or sweets. They seemed almost evil to him.

Now all he thought about was running. He ate, slept, and lived running. He never walked anywhere. He ran the stairs at his office, all ten flights of them, two or three times a day, and didn't even get winded.

Then, two days before he was to run his first ultra marathon, he was standing in a bank, the same bank, and had another heart attack.

And he found himself instantly back in the bakery from the first time he had died.

He knew at once what had happened.

The thick, rich smell of the fresh pastries and cookies hit him like a sledgehammer.

And just as when he left here the first time, he was so fat, he couldn't move.

But this time he didn't want to eat anything in the bakery. The smell was so thick it was almost nauseating.

What he really wanted was to get up and run.

But he couldn't.

He was far, far too fat from eating so much sweet stuff. He could no longer move.

So he screamed for help.

He just sat there, surrounded by cases of pies and cookies and cinnamon rolls, screaming for help.

No help came.

He knew he was dead again.

And all he wanted to do was go running.

Put in some miles.

But it seems he had died and gone to bakery heaven once again. And now he was paying for the first time he visited the special bakery.

He was paying for his inability to control himself.

He tried to move again, but his bulk kept him in the chair.

Maybe in a few days of not eating, he would be able to move.

He sat back and took a deep breath, hoping the air wasn't so full of calories that it kept him fat.

Not eating would do it.

And then he could start working off this weight, and get out of here and start running again.

Maybe find runners' heaven.

He imagined it to be a place of wide sidewalks and fresh air and people smiling and waving as he ran by.

He just had to starve himself enough.

And not be tempted by any of the cookies, pies, and cinnamon rolls surrounding him.

So he sat there for what seemed to be days and days, starving, still too heavy to move, and growing too weak to even try.

And even worse, all the sweets surrounding him were starting to smell really good.

Finally he decided he had to do something. He worked to rock himself out of the chair to stagger toward the cinnamon rolls.

He had almost made it when he woke up again.

He blinked twice and stared into the smiling face of a nurse, one of the same ones that had taken care of him after his first heart attack.

"Welcome back, Glen," the nurse said.

"Good to be back," Glen managed to choke out.

"You need to rest," she said. "I'll tell the doctor you are awake."

Glen nodded, then said softly, "Any chance I could get a cinnamon roll?"

The nurse laughed and smiled at him. "You know, that was the exact same thing you said when you woke up the last time you had a heart attack."

Glen just shuddered and closed his eyes.

And when he did, all he could see was that case of cinnamon rolls, so close, yet so, so far away.

Smith's
STORIES
DEAN WESLEY SMITH
SUBDIVISION SURVIVAL:
THE GAME
A Bryant Street Story

SUBDIVISION SURVIVAL: THE GAME

Billionaire J. R. Kuchar bought all seventy homes in an enclosed subdivision. Every home monitored completely and a massive fence, impossible to climb, protected the entire facility, with military guards on patrol.

Every house armed with the same weapons. Finally the most dangerous survival game ever invented started. **Subdivision Survival.**

Real life or game. All a person must do to win? Stay alive for a year.

The four-bedroom mini-mansion looked very similar, yet different from the one just over the hedge next door. Or the ones that lined the curving street.

Tile floors, open concept main area with a chef's-level

kitchen to one side. Floor-to-ceiling windows along the wall facing the backyard and the pool.

There had to be a formal dining room, of course, for those "special" occasions. It was off to one side of the kitchen and on the other side a dining nook with a table and six chairs that also looked out over the pool and got perfect morning light, or at least that was what the saleslady told him in her pitch.

Just like every house in this development, the fences around the backyard were high enough to ensure privacy.

There would be a guest suite down a hall on the main floor and up a grand staircase, two bedrooms and a master bedroom suite. Every house in the development similar.

A three-car garage, of course. And all the best finishes on the counters and bathroom fixtures were top of the line.

This house had been staged with actually tasteful furniture in brown and tan tones that lightened up the stark white and off-white of the tile and walls and the black appliances.

It even had two beds upstairs in the bedrooms.

"I'll take it," he said. "Staging furniture and all."

The saleslady nodded, trying not to show her joy at making a sale over the developer's asking price.

His name was J.R. Kuchar, although today he was buying this house as Chandler Church for one of his many companies, called Chandler Holdings, Inc. He didn't care what the home cost. He had far, far more money than he could ever spend, even buying a house every other day as he had been doing through all of his many companies as they came up for sale in this development.

In fact, as of this one, he owned all seventy in this gated development that sort of floated in the desert like a colorful oasis. None of the property around it had been developed yet and it wouldn't be since he owned all of that as well.

He had cleaning people cleaning all of the homes regularly, and yard crews doing all the lawns and pools. Everything was perfectly maintained.

And every house was empty.

Never lived in.

No one knew he owned them all, not even the developer who had built and sold them all. Every house had been bought by a different company, and he owned all the companies. All seventy of them.

So now, finally, he could get started. And that just made him smile like any new homeowner would smile.

Four days later he had a fencing crew put up a fifteen-foot-high fence around the entire subdivision. Not climbable. Razor wire along the top. Impossible to cut through or dig under.

His reasoning to get it approved was that the development sat in the middle of a desert and he wanted to keep unwanted visitors out. Of course, that was not the reason at all.

He replaced the security guard crew at the entrance with a dozen former-military mercenaries with real guns that fired real ammunition. And he built watch posts every hundred yards all the way around the development, most of them hidden in the desert.

No one was getting in or out of his subdivision without permission.

He then had every home completely wired with surveillance cameras and sound mikes. That took almost three months to do all seventy homes, plus furnish the ones he had bought without furniture and appliances.

Every camera was extremely well hidden and there was at least one in every room, including walk-in closets. Each had a mike.

And it was all connected to his mansion that sat on a hill a mile above this subdivision. There he had a forty-screen room with one chair on swivel right in the middle.

And in front of that chair a huge control board. From that room he could see every inch of both inside and outside of every home in his subdivision.

All seventy of them.

And every foot of the street as well.

He also had built on one wall in each home a massive gun rack. Every home had the exact same arsenal of weapons and ammunition. Real weapons, real ammunition.

Kuchar himself hated guns of any type, but they needed to be there as part of the game.

Finally J.R. Kuchar was almost ready.

With him watching through cameras, he had teams interview couples by yet another of his fake companies. The couples had applied from around the world to take part in the most dangerous survival game ever invented.

Subdivision Survival.

The rules were simple:

Seventy couples would be given a house to live in. They would own the house if they stayed through the entire year in the house.

Enough supplies would be stocked in each home for them to last for almost one year.

If the couple managed to still be alive and living in their assigned home after one year, they not only won the home, they would be given ten million dollars each. Twenty million per couple.

Over the year, a couple could leave at any time and win nothing. The home at the end of the game would go back on the market.

The prize pool was one billion, four hundred million and was sitting in escrow. For each couple who did not make it, the losing couple's share would be divided by the ones who did make it to the last day.

If one member of the couple left or died, the other member could still win their own share. In other words, even though they went in as couples, it was every person for themselves.

As an extra bonus, ten different packets of ten million dollars were hidden along the street in either front yards or in the common areas along the winding mile-long street. Everyone living in the subdivision would get one clue per week as to the location of the extra treasures.

Every house had shovels in their garages, as well as other tools they might need.

There would be no police or any medical help for the entire year.

If someone was injured or had a medical emergency and had to leave the subdivision, they were eliminated. They had to get to the front gate on their own. No ambulance would be allowed inside.

Regulars laws did apply if someone was caught breaking a law of any kind.

If the person was caught committing any crime such as breaking and entering or assault or murder, they could be arrested and disqualified at the end of the game.

But the police would not enter until after the last day finished. It would be up to the other homeowners to do the policing.

Three hundred and sixty-five days of *Subdivision Survival*.

With the interviews, Kuchar said no to a number of couples simply because they were not in good enough shape to make it. The food each couple would have would be running out around day three hundred unless they were careful. Each house was supplied with enough of the basics like toilet paper and such to last the same amount of time. Those last sixty-five days would get real interesting.

Plus, Kuchar had to be honest with himself. It was his money, he just didn't want to watch unattractive people for a year.

So most of the couples who applied were of two basic types. Survivalists and thrill-seekers. All were young, all in good shape, all driven by the money.

Perfect as far as Kuchar was concerned. Young couples fighting for their lives in an expensive home in a subdivision, just letting each day go by to get to a promised windfall.

Kuchar just laughed at the symbolism of that.

It took less than two weeks to get the seventy couples, plus two alternates in case a couple backed out at the last minute. No one did, so Kuchar's people gave the two extra couples five million and signed them to a nondisclosure agreement that took the money back if they said anything.

At midnight, New Year's Eve, seventy black limos with windows blacked out formed a line and went into the subdivision. Each limo had two armed guards with it.

Each limo pulled up to the front of a house and the couple unloaded their clothing and bathroom supplies into their new home. They were not allowed to bring anything else and all of them had been searched.

Within an hour, every limo was gone, the street empty, and every house in the subdivision had lights on and blinds closed.

Subdivision Survival had started. The only game that imitated real life in more ways than one. And brought out the best and the worst in people.

Only this time, instead of every couple in every subdivision playing their own game, seventy couples were playing the exact same game.

Instead of banks and mortgage companies watching, this time only one man would be paying attention. A man with more money than he would ever need and too much time on his hands. A man who grew up in a subdivision he hated, with neighbors who treated him like he didn't belong.

This subdivision and all the lives in it now belonged to J.R. Kuchar for no other reason than his amusement.

And he was in his big chair, in front of his many screens, ready to watch.

Smith's STORIES

DEAN WESLEY SMITH

THE WOMAN WHO KNEW THE TIME

A Bryant Street Story

THE WOMAN WHO KNEW THE TIME

On Bryant Street, really strange things happen. Usually they exist with a fantasy twist or a Twilight Zone feel.

But every-so-often other things happen. Science fiction things like time travel. Battling time travel.

With robbery. Yeah, only on Bryant Street.

———

ONE

Sally Lawrence had shoulder-length auburn hair. Not red, not brunette, auburn, like the fall leaves. The hair curled seemingly naturally over her collar, just touching her shoulders if she tilted her head one way or another.

She stood in front of me in the food court, in the line for Big Taco's Big Truck a block from the courthouse in downtown Boise. I could see a few freckles and a nifty small mole on her neck that appeared in and out of sight, taunting me.

The day was warm, not too hot, so she wore a light white blouse and carried a light Levi jacket over her arm with her blue purse. Her jeans and blue tennis shoes completed the casual afternoon outfit perfectly.

She had what I called a runner's body. Thin, in shape, and moved smoothly and easily.

I dressed almost identically to her, except my blouse was blue and my shoes had orange ties on them. I didn't carry a coat because I knew for a fact I wouldn't need it.

Without heels, I stood five-five and Sally was only an inch taller. I loved that. And I really wanted to run my fingers through her hair, but I knew there would be enough time for that if everything worked out as I hoped.

She didn't know I was standing behind her in line. She couldn't sense me there, even though I had been with her, following her car, since she left her home on Bryant Street. She should be more careful when out in the future, if she had a future here.

She reached the truck window and ordered and I enjoyed her rich voice, not too high, perfect for her short frame. And she laughed easily. And her smile always lit up her face.

I just loved watching her. I was completely in love with a woman I was following. Very, very unusual for me. I normally never became involved with my targets in any fashion.

Sally was special.

When she finished ordering and paying and stepped aside, she glanced at me and smiled lightly as I stepped up to the window and ordered. She was good, very good.

And very smooth.

She saw me, just not in the way I wanted and hoped for.

She had no idea that in one future I was destined to be her wife, her partner, living with her in that three-bedroom ranch she had just bought. At some point she would see me that way I hoped.

Maybe even today.

She got her food ahead of mine and moved to a shaded bench and table to eat. She worked about three blocks from here in an investment firm and on Tuesdays, like today, only went in after lunch, working from home in the morning.

I took my lunch, a large Big Taco Special, and with a nod to her as I passed her, headed down the street. We would see each other again very shortly.

Right after I saw her for the first time and discovered that she and I were destined to be together, I had bought the house across from hers on Bryant Street.

I ate my Big Taco Special at my desk in my office looking out over the city. I was only three blocks from the food court and today I had wished the walk to be longer, it was so nice.

In my office I had a person who answered phones for me named Dan in the outer office and another who kept track of my investments and did my books in a second office. Although I never let either of them actually touch the money or my computer or anything attached to me.

They had no idea that my income came from looking out just ahead in time, seeing what would be profitable, and then getting in ahead of the profit. I did it carefully and slowly and yet it still had made me a very rich woman.

That was my cover.

And it was with my special device that cut through time that I could also see that Sally and I would be an item, then a partnership.

What I called my invention in my cover was fairly simple, actually, and I had managed to hook it up to my laptop. My cover was that after a doctorate in mathematics from MIT, I had realized one fine spring day that scientists, including me, made things too complex.

So I just had worked to find a way to look between moments in time to see a possible future. A simple way.

Looking at the future was actually easy. It took no real power and I stored nothing in this office. My memory of what I saw was it. I could not allow even one bit to find its way off my private network. So to be safe, I flat recorded nothing ever. And destroyed my laptop every two weeks to be sure.

I played the game perfectly.

I could scan moments of time if I had the exact coordinates and time, so I brought up the food court ten minutes into the future. Sally was still there, just finishing her lunch.

As I watched, she tossed her garbage into a trash can, and then, while staring at her phone, stepped into the street and right in front of a delivery truck trying to beat a yellow light.

The sight of her lifeless body flying through the air made me sick to my stomach.

"Show time," I said out loud. I had seen what would happen in ten minutes.

I slammed out of the office at full run, purposefully leaving my computer up and running and made it the three blocks to the food court, coming in from the side, just as Sally stood.

She moved over to toss away her food and then looked at her phone to step into the street.

I grabbed her by the arm and yanked her back as the truck missed her by a foot.

Her wonderful brown eyes were wide in shock at how close she had come to dying.

"Thank you," she said, her voice almost a whisper.

"Damn phones will distract you every time," I said.

"Lucky you were here and not on your phone," she said, smiling.

"Glad to help," I said. "My name is Lena." I extended my hand.

"Sally," she said.

"Nice meeting you, neighbor," I said, smiling, my heart fluttering at our first conversation after all this time and the wonderful feel of her hand against mine.

"Neighbor?" Sally asked, frowning, still holding my hand.

"I bought the house on Bryant Street just across the

street from yours. The tan one. I saw you pulling out today."

"Oh, wow!" Sally said, now really beaming. "Never thought I would ever meet anyone in that neighborhood."

"Yeah," I said, "most of them are locked down pretty tight and very weird."

Sally laughed. "Well, I think I owe you a drink for saving my life. You work around here?"

"Got an office two blocks away in the Canary Building. Investment stuff."

Sally smiled again. "Three blocks away in the big tower there. Also investments. So you know Edwards Brewery?"

"Love the place," I said, and I did. "Best fries in the entire city."

I knew that was her plan, had seen it many times. And I loved it. How it ended was the difference.

"You got time tonight at six? Love to meet you there for that drink I owe you."

"Love to take you up on that," I said. "But the second round is on me."

She laughed and said "Deal."

I damn near melted. Her laugh could do that to anyone, let alone someone like me in love with her.

Then we both started to cross the street and I said, "You look that way, I'll look this way and maybe we can make it across this thing alive."

She laughed at that. "Teamwork. I love it."

After we separated, I almost floated back to my office. A wonderful day all the way around. I had a date with Sally.

And things were, after all this time, finally finishing up with my plan.

TWO

Sally went into her office, nodded to a few of the other workers in there in the bright, window-filled room. About thirty of them sat at fake-wood desks around the large area, some with clients. Sally had nothing to do with any of them, even though a few of them thought she did.

She then went through a private office with her name on the door and then into a private back room, hidden behind a bookcase that only she and her husband could access.

Craig sat at a bank of large computer screens, studying them. On two of them Sally could see Lena going into her office, smiling.

"Man, that woman is in love with you," Craig said, turning and smiling at Sally.

Sally just kissed him, then said, "She's nice and stunningly good looking. And the dummy accident trick worked like a charm. She thought she was saving me. And we have a date at Edwards tonight."

"I know," Craig said, pointing to one screen. "I've been pulling the event and setting it up and feeding it to her just in case she decides to look ahead."

"She will," Sally said. "She is very, very careful."

Craig nodded. "I also got her bank account information for her five main accounts while she was saving your life. I have access now to all of them and we can drain them at a moment's notice. There is a lot of money in there. Wow!"

"You got it?" Sally asked, now excited. They had been working for months to get Lena's financial information. They had to stage the fake rescue to not have her do her normal security on her system when she left. And it had worked.

"Got it all," Craig said. "And she can't track the fact that I am in there."

Sally nodded as she watched Lena go to work in her office again, doing exactly as they had expected her to do, look ahead to see the date tonight.

The woman really was in love with her. That was too bad. She was cute and it might have been fun.

Actually, it would have been a lot of fun, Sally had no doubt about that.

THREE

I loved how Sally's husband, Craig, set up the events of the date tonight with Sally. I admired him for that. Little did he know that if my plan worked, today would be the last time he would see his wife. But that would depend on Sally, of course. Free will often changed the future. This date had two very different outcomes and me and my people had seen them both.

I stayed in routine to not arouse any suspicion. A few minutes before I needed to I shut down my computer and all access to my bank accounts through it, then headed at a nice walk to Edwards.

The evening was still warm and I didn't carry anything but my small purse.

Edwards was one of those wonderful bars made of mostly polished wood and old timbers. It was massive and people could find tables easily that were private even if the place was packed.

The sound hit me as I entered. Talking and laughing and some country music in the background. Lots of people from offices all over Boise enjoying a drink and a snack before heading home. I had often come in here in the last year. I loved it.

A perfect place for Sally and my first date.

And it smelled wonderfully of French fries. The place always had that smell.

I stood off to one side for a few minutes, watching, until Sally came in and gave me a big smile.

I was bold enough to hug her lightly. "How are you doing after your close call?"

She smiled. "Feeling lucky."

I knew what she was really talking about. Her husband, Craig, was about to take the bait I had planted over the last year to catch them. He would drain all my money, all the while being recorded and trapped by my people that had been set up fifty years in the future to monitor all time-travel crime.

But Sally might end up lucky in another way, if I was lucky.

We sat in a private booth near the back and sheltered from most of the sounds of others. We sat close together and I had no doubt she really liked me. Not as much as I loved her, but she liked me and for now I would take that much.

Finally, after we both had had two drinks and were touching each other's hands a lot, I reached into my purse and sat a small cube on the table. It was ceramic and totally white.

"What's that?" Sally asked.

"Time block," I said. "Allows us to be completely private, with no one watching in either from the past or the future."

Sally pretended confusion.

"My name really is Lena. And I am a Time Enforcement Detective from just over a hundred years in the future."

"A what?" Sally asked.

I just went forward, not daring to stop now.

"We have been tracking you and your husband now for the last two years, and as we speak, your husband is being arrested for taking the funds from my dummy accounts set up to bait him. He will be taken back to your normal time period thirty years in the future, tried in a secret time court and put in jail for a very long time."

Sally just looked at me with a mixture of fear and anger. Her wonderful brown eyes were slits, her face frozen, yet I still found her fantastically beautiful.

"I have been allowed to make you a deal," I said.

"Go on," Sally said.

"You can join me, be my partner, at first in a probationary status. You would need to divorce your husband in your original time period, and live with me and work with me here to capture others like you and your husband. There are many thieves from times in the future invading this period of time for the very reasons you and your husband chose it."

Sally just looked at me like I was completely crazy. She sat there, breathing slowly, clearly trying to catch her bearings. Another reason I wanted her at my side. She was level under pressure.

After a long moment, she said, "Why would you do this for me?"

"Your husband said it clearly when you went back into your office this afternoon."

"You were watching us?"

"Of course we were," I said. "We have watched your every move now for almost six months as you worked to get my bait money. We all admitted that your plan was very, very smart. The fake accident was brilliant. So do you remember what your husband said about me when you returned?"

Sally nodded. "He said you were in love with me."

"And I am," I said. "And I have enough pull in the force to save you from jail time and try you out as my partner. The lover side of things we'll take as we go along, if you are interested."

"I am interested in that part, no doubt," Sally said. "Back in school I always tended to like women more than men."

I didn't tell her that I knew that. My heart just fluttered and I took a sip of my drink to stay calm.

"But I know nothing of being a cop," she said.

"Neither do I, really," I said. "Basically, what we do is just the same thing you and your husband were trying to do, only better and in reverse. We set you up like you tried to set me up."

"And then what happens? What is happening to Craig right now?"

My team calls in the police side of the Time Enforcement Service, they arrest him, we supply them with all the documentation. The police will take him and the documentation back to your time and he will have a speedy trial."

"How long will he be in jail?"

"Maybe fifteen to twenty years," I said. "He will have time to have a life once he is out, I am sure."

"So my choice is to go to jail or work with you?"

I shook my head no. "You have been given a probation for your part in this crime simply because of this offer, no matter if you accept it or not. If you don't accept it, you will be taken back to your time and monitored for any future unlawful time activity. Nothing more. You will be free to live your life as you want. And if you really love Craig, you can wait for him."

"Do I have any time to think about this?" Sally asked.

"When I remove that cube from the table, your time will be up," I said. "But let me ask you this. Did you enjoy the thrill of trying to trap me more than you would have enjoyed the money?"

Sally nodded. "I did, actually."

"Then you would love this job. It is all that. Playing roles, outsmarting very smart people. Fantastic fun."

"And you said we would stay here, in this time period?"

I waved my hand around at the wonderful bar we were sitting in, the distant sounds of laughter and music. "Not torture, that's for sure."

She smiled for the first time since I revealed myself.

"So, you are setting me free either way, no matter what?"

I nodded. "Your choice is to go back to your normal time and live free or to come and work with me in the Time Enforcement Agency trying to stop people like you and your husband. And we do get paid, by the way. All expenses."

"Like those homes on Bryant Street?"

I nodded.

She sat for a moment, then she looked up into my eyes. "Thank you."

I said nothing. I didn't know if there would be a "but" coming after that or not.

She leaned closer to me and said softly, "I need to test one thing?"

"What's that?" I asked, loving her breath being so close to me.

She leaned closer and kissed me, softly at first, then I responded and the kiss went on for a wonderfully long time.

Finally she pulled away, smiling, her light skin flushed. I

was sure my skin was as well. That kiss had been really something.

"I'm thinking I want to stay and learn how to work for the Time Patrol, or whatever you called it."

I beamed. "Time Enforcement Agency."

"Whatever," she said. Then she said "Thank you" one more time before kissing me again.

And it was better than the first time around, which boded real well for our future on Bryant Street.

BRYANT STREET

Smith's
STORIES
DEAN WESLEY SMITH
ENJOYING THE COMPANY
A Bryant Street Story

ENJOYING THE COMPANY

Paul Tegner's plan seems simple. Murder his wife, Helen, and bury her in the back yard under the patio.

Nothing to it.

But Paul forgot what street he lived on, and how nothing ever works out as planned on Bryant Street.

————

Paul Tegner dropped the nude body of his wife from his wheelbarrow onto a blue plastic tarp used for painting that he had laid out on the garage floor. She hit with a resounding thud and a crack that was her head hitting the hard concrete.

Paul had used the tarp just a week ago, so some of the paint on it was still sticky and as Helen rolled over from the fall, she got white splotches on her right hip, right boob, and right knee.

Paul just sort of laughed and went to the workbench along the back wall of his garage and opened the can of white paint and slopped some all over Helen, leaving a large splash for her face and hair. She had hated getting dirty and anything sticky would send her into panic attacks.

She wasn't panicking now. The claw on the back of his hammer to the side of her skull had made sure she would never panic about anything again.

And the woman who had wanted him to make sure everything around their new home on Bryant Street was perfect was now going to live in eternity with white paint all over her naked body. He thought that wonderfully perfect and ironic.

He put the paint can back on the bench and closed it tight, then went to Helen. She was a beautiful woman with a beautiful body, of that there was no doubt. But the beauty had gone no deeper than her skin and the layers of makeup she used every morning.

Underneath the beauty she was cold, calculating, and just flat abusive.

And even more amazing, he had put up with it for five long years. Right up until tonight when he asked for a divorce, she said no one was ever going to divorce her. After all, what would people think?

So she had then gone into her ignoring him routine, as if he was no greater than a slug. So he had simply gone out to his workbench, gotten his carpenter's claw hammer, and buried the claw part into her skull at least three inches deep.

Instant divorce and no one would ever be the wiser, since no one would know except for what he would tell them.

He carefully wrapped her up, making sure no white paint got on the garage floor.

Then he put layers of duct tape around the tarp to hold it in position.

Then he took another blue painting tarp and opened it on the floor beside her and rolled her over on top of it and did the same thing again, sealing every seam as best he could.

Then he hefted her back into the wheelbarrow and rolled her over against the wall and parked her, putting a couple shovels in the wheelbarrow beside her.

You could never tell there was a body in the big pile of blue tarp. Just looked like some sort of gardening project.

And it was.

Then he turned off the garage light, spent the next hour cleaning up the blood from where he had hit her in her bedroom. They had long ago stopped sleeping in the same room. Seemed he snored.

Then right on time for their normal bedtime, he clicked off the lights and went to bed.

Just as always he got up and made coffee, but this morning, instead of taking a cup into her bedroom because she demanded it, he just sat and read the morning news on his laptop and ate a bagel and drank his coffee. Outside, the day looked like it was going to be a perfect day, temps in the low seventies, all sun.

So about ten, he headed out to the backyard with his shovel and started digging a long trench to the west side of his concrete patio. It was pretty easy digging, since they had had a wet spring. And after a break for lunch, he had the trench a good twenty feet long and about two feet deep.

He had been planning on planting a row of hedge trees and actually had them sitting beside the house on the left.

So he went and got a couple of them and planted two close together in his trench. They were fast-growing and would by next summer provide wonderful, natural shade for the patio.

That was enough for one day, so he went back inside, took a shower, and cooked himself a wonderful steak dinner with fries. And he even allowed himself one beer. He figured he deserved it.

The next morning at ten he was back out in the trench, only this time he went deeper right in the middle, digging a hole down and under the concrete patio. He knew that right at this spot there were no power or water or sewer lines because he had built the patio back when he was married to his first wife, Alice. So he knew he could go down into the ground as far as he wanted.

After a lunch break, he kept working and ended up with a pretty good-sized cave under the patio.

At that point he went into the garage and got his wheelbarrow with Helen's wrapped-up body and hauled it out to the hole and dumped it in.

Then he got down in the hole with her and made sure she was as far back under the concrete as he could get her, then he filled the hole back in, really packing the dirt up under the concrete over her body.

He even put in four six-foot two-by-four pieces of lumber up against the underside of the concrete to give it more support when her body decomposed and left a hole. Last thing he needed was for Helen to cause a crack in Alice's perfect concrete patio.

He planted four more of the trees before finally calling it a day and going in for a shower and dinner.

He finished the project by lunch the next day and wow did those trees look great along that side of the patio.

Then he went down to a local nursery and got a bunch of flowering plants and planted the flowers under the trees. That was really going to be beautiful next year for the new tenants to enjoy.

Since Helen had no job and no real friends, no one asked where she had gone. He was ready to tell people who asked that they had decided to divorce and she was traveling. But no one asked, just as no one had asked about Alice, his first wife, either.

Four weeks later, he filed divorce papers and since he was so good at her signature before she had suddenly died, he signed the papers for her.

In the divorce she got everything she had brought into

the marriage, which was basically her clothes and an old Buick, which he sold four days later.

He had a lot of family money and in the divorce she laid no claim to his money. Nicest thing she ever did in her entire life. In reality, she had loved spending his money. Hated him, but loved his money and figured she would get it when he died.

Just like Alice. Wow, he really could pick wives. Zero for two so far.

After the no-fault divorce was final, he found himself a place to live downtown and put the house on Bryant Street up for sale. He had been there long enough with Alice and then Helen. He liked the place but he needed to start over.

He sold off all of the furniture and Helen's clothing, and kept a few of his own tools, including the big claw hammer to remember Helen and a screwdriver to remember April.

The house sold quickly and the new tenants loved the patio and set up a large barbeque right over Helen's body.

But about a month later he got a call from the new tenant.

"Did you ever see anything strange on the patio?" the tenant asked.

He said he hadn't and the tenant went on to tell him how two naked women, one covered in white paint, had been sitting on their patio furniture last night and then just vanished.

Paul just shook his head. Helen was under once side of the patio, Alice the other. Paul offered to the new tenant that if the problem wouldn't go away, Paul would just buy the place back.

So two months later, Paul Tegner moved back into his home on Bryant Street. This time he decorated the house to his tastes, including a massive television screen filling most of one wall in the living room.

He spent the next month building a higher fence around his entire backyard so no neighbors could see his patio.

Then he put three chairs, a small table near one chair, and a barbeque on the patio.

And every nice evening during the spring, summer, and fall, right after dark, he cooked himself a steak and potato on the grill and had dinner with his previous two wives.

Unlike when they were alive, they didn't talk.

They didn't abuse him and belittle him or put him down in any way. They didn't demand he do things he didn't want to do. And they also didn't want to spend his money, which he found perfect.

They just sat there naked, staring at him as he ate.

And even more than he remembered, they were both very attractive women.

Especially silent, dead, and naked.

A situation that could only be found in the backyards and on the patios of Bryant Street.

DEAN WESLEY SMITH

NOT EASY TO KILL
THE LIGHT NEXT DOOR

A Bryant Street Story

NOT EASY TO KILL THE LIGHT NEXT DOOR

Very strange things happen on Bryant Street.

For Cayden Cavanaugh, getting rid of a light to guard the neighborhood became his passion.

He thought of nothing else.

A simple story of a light and a man with passion. But on Bryant Street, nothing remains simple for long.

———————

Cayden Cavanaugh was done.

Fed up.

Last straw.

Over his limit.

And every other damn cliché a person could think of.

The light had to go.

And he would make it go. That stupid white light

towering over Bob and Stephie's garage had cost him sleep, his job, his wife, and most of his money. In a few days it would cost him this house.

The light would pay.

And it would pay tonight.

He should have done this long ago.

Cayden sat at the table in his once beautiful and modern suburban kitchen. His former wife Hanna had insisted on the best white granite counters, the most expensive light-blue glass-tile backsplash, and top range steel appliances when they built this dream home. He had loved every bit of it.

Now he could only see those things by the light mounted above the garage next door. He had no money to pay the power bill and the power had been turned off three days ago.

But Cayden could see enough from the light next door to load the pistol he had bought two days before.

Tonight the light would pay.

The sink was full of unwashed dishes and they smelled like rotten fish, but Cayden no longer cared. Hanna was long gone and he would be soon. He couldn't hold off the bank any longer. They were taking the dream home, taking everything, and all because of that stupid light.

And even leaving the house, moving to another city, another country, he knew he would never escape that light. He had to finish this once and for all right now, tonight.

Things had been fine just a short year before.

Then at one summer neighborhood barbeque Bob had

told him he was putting in a security light on his garage, on a pole sticking up from the garage peak. Bob said it would cost a bunch, but it would make his house safer and also the entire area.

Cayden had thought it a wonderful idea.

How stupid had he been?

So three weeks later, when the light first clicked on as the sun set, Cayden was stunned at how bright it was. So bright that it seemed to fill every room in Cayden and Hanna's house with a dull white light that washed out all the colors they had so carefully picked.

He and Hanna took to closing the blinds at night, but for Cayden the light still seemed to fill everything. It felt like a disease eating away at something that had once been beautiful.

Hanna said she didn't much notice the light with the blinds pulled, but Cayden hated it with a passion. As far as he was concerned, the light was ruining everything they had built.

A month later they put up those room-darkening blinds for their bedroom and the rooms on the side of the house facing Bob and Stephie's home. At that point Cayden was having trouble sleeping and getting more and more angry at the slightest things.

But most especially at all the light and how it washed everything out.

The darkening shades didn't seem to help, even though Hanna said the room was pitch black.

It wasn't pitch black.

The light was there.

Cayden could see it.

He could feel it.

It kept him awake.

He knew it attacked the walls of his home like a tiny army never letting up. It was always right outside the window, right against the walls, flooding the roof, trying to get in at the slightest mistake on his part.

He wasn't sure why Hanna couldn't see the gray in how the light out there was so strong it took even total blackness and robbed it of power.

Two months after the light first came on, Cayden went to Bob and asked him to take it down. Cayden said he would even pay for the cost of the light.

Bob said it made him and Stephie feel safer, so he refused.

A month later Cayden and Bob got into a fight over the light and Cayden slugged Bob. Actually it seems that he did more than just slug him, although Cayden didn't remember most of it he was so angry. Turns out he put Bob in the hospital and Bob pressed charges.

Cayden spent two nights in jail and still had his case pending for trial.

Then Cayden found himself yelling more and more at Hanna and finally three months ago she left to go live with her parents. She begged him to get professional help.

He knew he was fine.

It was all the light's fault.

The light was eating at him.

At work, about the time Hanna left, Cayden noticed the light had followed him to work, that it was washing out all the colors in his office. He started working with the lights off and the blinds pulled to try to block out the light, but it still got in.

He got angrier and angrier.

The light had now infected everything.

A week later he lost his job.

His boss told him to get help.

Cayden knew he was fine. He didn't know why everyone kept telling him to get help, that he wasn't his old self. He knew he would be fine as soon as he got rid of the light.

Tonight he would do just that.

Finally.

Cayden looked around at the dark kitchen, a room that had many good memories. He was going to miss this home as much as he missed Hanna.

Then he made sure the gun was loaded and stood. It was time to face the devil.

Once he had won, maybe he and Hanna could start over, plan a new life in a new home, away from the light.

Maybe get some color back in their lives.

Holding the now loaded pistol in his right hand, he went out the back door into the yard that seemed so bright it could be daylight. The gun felt extra heavy, far heavier than it had felt in the store when he bought it.

That evil light above Bob and Stephie's garage seemed

to flood his entire yard, washing out the wonderful shades of darkness with a pale, white world of blandness.

His barbeque no longer looked black, but a light gray. The green grass looked almost pink. The dark, oak-stained fence seemed like it had been painted dull white.

The light was so powerful it leached all the color out of everything, just as it had leached away his life.

He turned toward the fence to get closer to the light and then realized it felt like he was walking upstream against rushing water.

The light knew what he was planning and wanted to stop him.

He would not stop.

He had to win this fight.

He leaned into the light, focusing on the sidewalk in front of him with every step, the gun in his hand getting heavier and heavier.

Now it felt like he was in a strong wind that seemed to get stronger and stronger with each step.

And the light got brighter, if that was possible.

He finally stopped and planted both feet firmly. Then he looked up at the light.

It blinded him like looking into the sun.

The pain was intense, filling his entire head.

He wanted to scream in agony, but somehow he managed to raise the pistol and fire at the white light above him.

The sound was so loud it shocked him. It echoed over the neighborhood and a dog barked.

He staggered back, the pain in his head worse.

The light still blinded him.

He couldn't let it win that easily.

He fired at it again.

And then again.

He heard glass shattering, but the light was still as bright, if not brighter.

He fired over and over until finally the gun clicked empty and he dropped it.

He then sat down, his back to the light, shaking.

The light had won.

Everything around him was still washed out of all color and his eyes burnt from looking into the brightness.

The pain in his head radiated out like someone was poking sharp sticks into his eyes.

He finally just lay down, staring upward into the white light. He was in too much pain and too tired to move.

The light had won.

He was not sure how long it was until the police arrived and led him to the police car.

He could barely see any of it because of the bright light and the stabbing pain in his head.

By the time he reached the station he could only see white, with wonderful blackness around the edges.

A short time later he found himself in the hospital with a police guard. A young-sounding doctor was trying to shine a light into his eyes.

But Cayden couldn't see the light.

Or the doctor for that matter.

The blackness had slowly crept in from the sides of his vision until finally, thankfully, everything was black.

Everything.

The light was gone.

He had finally killed it.

He could finally sleep.

The next thing he heard was Hanna talking with a doctor. They were talking about him and an operation it seemed he had had.

Around him machines beeped and there were sounds of others talking out in the hallway.

The intense pain in his head was gone replaced by a dull ache and everything was blissfully black.

It felt wonderful to hear Hanna's voice again. Calming, not at all like the last time he had talked with her. He couldn't remember now why he had been so angry.

"We got the tumor completely," the doctor told Hanna. "But we don't think his vision will ever return I'm afraid. Just too much damage."

Cayden wanted to smile, to shout for joy, but instead he just lay there, not moving.

Blackness was fine by him.

The blackness was a victory.

He had fought the light and he had won and that was all that mattered.

He never wanted to see light again.

In blackness maybe he could live again.

Dean Wesley Smith

USA *Today* Bestselling Writer

Me and Beans and Great Big Melons

A Grocery Store Romance

ME AND BEANS AND GREAT BIG MELONS

When Innis went shopping to get ready for the Packers-Rams game, he never expected to meet one of them aliens.

But he also never expected to meet a woman who ate beans either. A strange supermarket romance. Are there any others when you live on Bryant Street?

———

I have never thought, wondered, or even pondered the idea of having a supermarket love affair. If I had, I certainly wouldn't have thought it would start and end in front of the green beans. I'm the kind of guy who really doesn't eat green beans, red beans, black beans, or any other color bean. I'm not prejudiced in my bean selection. I pretty much just hate them all equally.

And I flat don't understand how anyone could even eat the things.

I met my supermarket lover as I tried to figure out which Hamburger Helper would work for the night. I was an expert in Hamburger Helpers and all the different incarnations of the stuff. I could almost make it without looking at the box. Almost.

"Excuse me," a soft, husky voice said.

I jerked around, realizing that my cart and my body had made an effective roadblock in the aisle. And I hadn't even set up any detour signs.

A woman stood there with one of those yellow baskets for small amounts of stuff. Just like me, she was wearing jeans and a blue tee-shirt, but unlike me she also had a brown purse over her shoulder.

The purse, oddly enough, accented the wonderful color of her hair. I wondered if she had bought the purse because of that, or changed the color of her hair to match the purse. It was a question I would never think to ask any woman, even a woman I didn't know.

But yet, for some reason, she had made me think of it. I made a note to myself mentally to write down the weird supermarket moment. I hoped to be a writer in the future, when I could find the time, and often made notes about things that might come in handy in a story some day.

I found myself attracted to this woman wanting to get past me, and I did an instant inventory of her appearance.

Before I was laid off down at Sears, I had done lots of inventories of the warehouse, and had become known as

"Innis, the Inventory King." I had decided one day to practice the same craft on women I met, and grocery stores were great places, full of inventory.

Using my skills, I instantly looked her over while moving my cart out of her way. She wore a loose blue tee-shirt with nothing written on it, tight jeans, and expensive tennis shoes. Total inventory cost of two hundred bucks. She had on no jewelry at all, not even an earring. She was an easy inventory subject.

Miss Brown-Hair-Yellow-Basket: Two hundred bucks.

"Sorry," I said, as I finished my inventory and cart moving at the same time, leaving the cart in front of the green beans, never thinking that she might actually be trying to get to that area. If I didn't eat green beans, no one else did I was sure.

My first wife had called that self-centered-universe attitude my defining characteristic. I had considered that a compliment and still do.

"No problem," the brown-haired, two-hundred-dollar-woman said, giving me a wonderful, bright smile as she moved past me. The aroma of fresh soap caught me and I stared at her from behind for a moment, first watching her long hair move against her matching purse, then her ass under her tight jeans.

I had always been an ass man, staring at woman's asses before any other body part if the chance arose. This woman had a stareable ass, of that there was no doubt. Really tight.

A stareable tight ass wasn't worth anything on my inventory list, but it should be.

She walked a few steps and stopped, looking at the canned vegetables.

I went back to trying to decide which Hamburger Helper to pick to eat while the football game was on tonight. Packers against the Rams. Could be a real shouter.

"Sorry to bother you again," she said from behind me.

I turned around to look into the deepest green eyes I had seen in a long time. If all women had eyes like her, I would shift to being an eye-man instead of an ass-man.

She pointed at the bean section that my cart was blocking.

"Oh, sorry," I said, moving to pull the cart out of her way for the second time. "I didn't think anyone ate that stuff."

She laughed. "Usually I like my beans fresh. But when I can't get them fresh, I make do with canned."

Usually I'm not real honest with the women I meet, but this woman ate beans and had annoyed me by making me move my cart twice in the middle of my Hamburger Helper shopping. So I said the first thing that came to mind.

"I'm that way with women," I said. "When I can't find the fresh stuff, I resort to the canned as well."

She stared at me for a moment.

I returned her stare.

The faint store music went away; the sounds of the other shoppers went away. It was a movie moment.

Of course, I had no doubt this movie moment was going to end with the woman walking off in a huff. At least then I could watch her ass and get back to my shopping.

But she surprised me.

Suddenly her smile returned, followed by the richest, deepest laugh I had heard in a long time. It echoed off the cans of corn and surrounded me, pushing me back against the shelf of Hamburger Helper.

"Now that's an opening line I've never heard before," she said after she caught a breath from the laughter.

"Opening for what?" I asked.

She smiled. "My legs."

I looked her right in the eye. "Now tell me why I would want to get between the legs of a woman who eats beans?"

Again I was serious, and again she stared at me, stunned into a second movie moment right there on aisle four.

Then she damned near lost a lung laughing that wonderful laugh of hers. I guess to her I was a real laugh-a-minute kind of guy.

She finally caught her breath and stared at me, her bright smile lighting up everything.

"Well?" I asked. "I'm waiting for my reason."

"Because," she said, "beans go well with franks at a picnic."

She stepped forward and grabbed my crotch, never letting her green-eyed gaze drop from mine.

She rubbed me through my jeans a few times as again we were having a movie moment, only this time it was a sex scene right there in front of the Hamburger Helper. I doubted I was ever going to be able to eat Hamburger Helper without a hard-on again.

"I assume little Frank here wouldn't mind a picnic in the park."

"His name is Ben," I said as she kept rubbing. "Big Ben. And he likes melons on his picnics."

"I think that could be arranged," she said, rubbing one small, tight breast against my arm. Whatever she had thought, that wasn't a melon. More like an apple.

"Any other menu items?" she asked.

Any man with a woman rubbing his crotch on aisle four of a grocery store might have trouble answering a question like that. I didn't. "A television to watch the game while I eat."

Her hand came away from my crotch like Big Ben had lit a match and burnt her. She stared at me, then said, "My ex-husband would have rather watched television than make love to me."

"Did he like Hamburger Helper?" I asked, adjusting Ben a little to ease the tension of tight underwear.

"Yeah," she said, clearly upset at my request for a television at her picnic.

"Figures," I said.

Now she was starting to get angry. A moment ago she was offering me a picnic, basket, apples, and all. Now she was mad. I had never had a woman mad at me on aisle four in a grocery store before. Two things new in one day, both on the same aisle. I would really have to write this down for the story I would do some day.

"And why does it *figure*?" she demanded, as if I owed

her an answer just because she had given Big Ben a quick rubbing.

I shrugged. "You eat beans."

She made a choking sound, grabbed two cans of green beans, held them up for me to see like she was giving me the finger, put them in her little yellow basket, and walked off.

I watched her ass until she turned the corner and disappeared toward aisle five. Because her ass was so nice and tight, and her hand had felt so good on Big Ben, I thought for a moment about following her. But I knew there was nothing I could say to her to calm her down.

Besides, she ate beans. I hated beans, and no amount of Big Ben rubbing was going to erase that difference.

Also, if I spent time dealing with her over on aisle five, it might carry on to aisle six, and then even into the frozen food section on aisle eight, and if that happened I might miss the opening kick-off.

No bean-eating woman with a nice ass was worth missing the kick-off to a Packers-Rams game. Even if she had offered Ben an offer he had trouble refusing.

It seemed that my supermarket love affair had started and ended on aisle four.

I went back to trying to figure out which Hamburger Helper to get, finally picked up just the standard, and headed for aisle two where the Pabst Blue-Ribbon Beer lived and breathed and waited for me. No Hamburger Helper football game dinner was complete without Pabst.

I turned the corner onto the aisle. There was a short woman with a nice ass and short red hair parked right in front of the Pabst. She was studying the beer on the other side of the aisle as if reading labels would make the stuff any better.

I knew right off she was an alien, off one of them big ships from some other planet that had landed a year or so ago. All the alien women that I had seen on Fox News had short, bright-red hair and great bodies.

There had been hundreds of thousands of them, and all the countries of the world welcomed them to live. After awhile, they weren't even headlines anymore unless one of them got drunk and punched a cop or something.

The aliens had said they had come in friendship and just wanted to learn about us, but I had read stuff, and I knew better. More than likely they were going to kidnap us all and take us away and make dinner out of us.

But still, alien or not, she was standing in front of the Pabst and I had a game to watch.

"Excuse me," I said.

She turned to look at me, a puzzled look on her very human but very alien face.

Her dark eyes were like magnets, swirling pink and orange and brown. They held me with some unseen force. She was dressed in jeans and a blue tee-shirt, just like I was. Just like Miss Brown Hair had been. Only instead of apples in the tee-shirt orchard, she sprouted the biggest melons I had ever seen, especially for an alien as short as she was.

I did a quick inventory. Same as Miss-Brown-Purse. Two

hundred bucks. It seemed it was two-hundred-dollar-woman-day in the supermarket.

"Yes?" she asked. "Can I help you?"

Very formal, like the secretary at my doc's office. But oh, Miss-Alien-With-Melons' voice could melt grease in a cold frying pan.

I pointed to the beer. "Hamburger Helper and a hand job are never complete without Pabst."

For some reason it was my day to be honest with women. And aliens it seemed. Maybe someone had put something in the grocery store air to make me do it. Or maybe it was the excitement of a good football game that was causing it. I would have to think about it later, after the game, if I could stay awake long enough to do so.

She kept staring at me, then slowly smiled as she moved aside. "Aren't you forgetting one thing?" she asked.

"What's that?" I asked, figuring an insult to be next out of her mouth. Something about the rudeness of humans in social situations and that we all needed alien training or something. I grabbed my half case of beer and placed it next to the Hamburger Helper.

"A good Packers-Rams game."

Now it was my turn to stare at her like she was a winning lotto ticket. I didn't know alien women watched American football. Fox News had never mentioned anything like that. Maybe there was hope for all of us after all.

So, with that encouragement, I went ahead and asked the all-important question.

"Do you eat beans?"

She made a face. "Are you kidding? No human or alien should eat those things."

"Good," I said. "How's your ass?"

She turned around to show me, then said, "Engineered to be as tight as they make them. How's your big fella?"

"Big," I said.

She smiled and I smiled back.

I loved those alien eyes.

Then after my third or fourth movie moment of the shopping trip, this time right there in front of the beer, I stuck out my hand. "I'm Innis. I count things and hope to write stories."

She took my hand, her smooth skin sending wonderful warm sensations through my body right there in the cold beer section.

"Here on your planet, in your language, I'm called Melody," she said. "I'm not from around here. I rub things and hope to paint things. And if we don't hurry we're going to miss the kick-off. How big is your screen?"

Her eyes seemed to swirl and she smiled with that question.

"Sixty inches," I said, proud of the moment I could say that to an alien woman.

She smiled even wider and then reached down and touched Big Ben through my jeans. "Sixty inches, huh? Mind if I join you? I'll buy the hamburger."

"Deal," I said, enjoying the fact that Ben was getting a work-out right there in the supermarket.

She put a second half-case of Pabst in my cart, left her empty cart in front of the other beer, and helped me push mine to the meat section, letting one of her wonderful large melons rub firmly against my hand.

It pleased me that she hadn't intended on sharing my Pabst. I really had to know a woman, or an alien for that matter, before I let that happen. Even if she was sharing her melons.

On the way past aisle six, we passed Miss Brown-Hair-And-Matching-Purse, who gave me a very, very long and angry look.

"Wow, what is her problem?" Melody asked, turning with me to watch the angry woman walk away. "Besides the fact that she has a tight ass."

"Very tight," I said, agreeing. "But she hates football and eats beans."

"Oh, that explains it," Melody said, shaking her head. "One of my people's biggest puzzles about your planet is how anyone could eat beans. They are poison to us. It may be a mystery we will never solve."

I was starting to really like these aliens.

"Let me know if you do," I said.

"The moment we figure it out," she said, laughing a high laugh that sounded very off-worldish. With that, me and my first alien supermarket lover headed for the check-out counter and a Hamburger Helper football game.

NEWSLETTER SIGN-UP

Follow Dean on BookBub

Be the first to know!
Just sign up for the Dean Wesley Smith newsletter, and keep up with the latest news, releases and so much more—even the occasional giveaway.

So, what are you waiting for? To sign up go to deanwesleysmith.com.

But wait! There's more. Sign up for the WMG Publishing newsletter, too, and get the latest news and releases from all of the WMG authors and lines, including Kristine Kathryn Rusch, Kristine Grayson, Kris Nelscott, *Pulphouse Fiction Magazine*, *Smith's Monthly*, and so much more.
To sign up go to wmgpublishing.com.

ABOUT THE AUTHOR

DEAN WESLEY SMITH

Considered one of the most prolific writers working in modern fiction, with more than 30 million books sold, *USA Today* bestselling writer Dean Wesley Smith published far more than a hundred novels in forty years, and hundreds of short stories across many genres.

At the moment he produces novels in several major series, including the time travel Thunder Mountain novels set in the Old West, the galaxy-spanning Seeders Universe series, the urban fantasy Ghost of a Chance series, a super-hero series starring Poker Boy, and a mystery series featuring the retired detectives of the Cold Poker Gang.

His monthly magazine, *Smith's Monthly*, which consists of only his own fiction, premiered in October 2013 and offers readers more than 70,000 words per issue, including a new and original novel every month.

During his career, Dean also wrote a couple dozen *Star Trek* novels, the only two original *Men in Black* novels, Spider-Man and X-Men novels, plus novels set in gaming and television worlds. Writing with his wife Kristine Kathryn Rusch under the name Kathryn Wesley, he wrote the novel for the NBC miniseries The Tenth Kingdom and other books for *Hallmark Hall of Fame* movies.

He wrote novels under dozens of pen names in the worlds of comic books and movies, including novelizations of almost a dozen films, from *The Final Fantasy* to *Steel* to *Rundown*.

Dean also worked as a fiction editor off and on, starting at Pulphouse Publishing, then at *VB Tech Journal*, then Pocket Books, and now at WMG Publishing, where he and Kristine Kathryn Rusch serve as series editors for the acclaimed *Fiction River* anthology series.

For more information about Dean's books and ongoing projects, please visit his website at www.deanwesley-smith.com and sign up for his newsletter.

For more information:
www.deanwesleysmith.com

f facebook.com/deanwsmith3

P patreon.com/deanwesleysmith

BB bookbub.com/authors/dean-wesley-smith